Indifferent to
trudged to the rig
house. The combination welder/generator unit
was mounted between the rig engine, rig draw
works and the back of the truck cab. He reached
for a welding helmet and put it on, tightening
the nut on the ratcheting headband. He paused.
He'd gotten the strangest feeling someone was
there watching. "Odd," he thought.... He pushed
the rubber-encased start button to warm up the
three hundred amp welder....

His hand grabbed the diamond plate catwalk
for balance and was forcibly seized in a fiery jolt.

ZAP! ....

*It looked like a routine well-drilling job. But
something, or someone, doesn't want Big Jim Bruno
to find water.*

Christmas 94.
To Cindy from, Mike M.

WITCHER

by
Bill Fry

WITCHER
© 1996 Bill Fry

ISBN: 0-9653259-0-3

Fried Publications
Homer, Alaska

Happy Birthday Mom.
I know you haven't read this one.

dows\er' (dou'zer) n. A person who uses a divining rod, willow branch, or other device to locate water, minerals, or other natural resources. [origin unknown]

di\vin\ing rod, stick, or wand (d vi' ning), a forked stick believed by some to be useful in locating water, oil, minerals, metals, and other things underground by dipping downward over a deposit of the substance sought.

1985 WORLD BOOK DICTIONARY, PG. 616

CHAPTER ONE

Yaku was a shaman who, during the course of serving his community, accumulated great wealth. He kept four wives, inhabited the most spacious dwelling, and controlled nearly all the trading in Point Hope.

It was widely known that in separate instances Yaku had murdered three men. He had killed others in battle. His imposing physical size and strength, along with his reputation as a shaman that delighted in the sight of flowing blood, terrified the Eskimo villagers of this Arctic settlement on the west coast of Alaska. It was also well known Yaku would not hesitate to use the dark medicine.

He came to Point Hope an orphaned Athabascan Indian, just over two years old. Reluctantly, the villagers agreed to take the child in at the urging of the nomad hunter who found him, cold and starving. The boy's parents were frozen to death but were still providing enough cover to keep him alive until the nomad came upon them at the banks of the Noatak River.

The great and wise one, Anuk, who had but one son, Kivuk, adopted the orphan. Anuk named him Yaku, "orphan traveler." Anuk proclaimed Yaku was to become second apprentice medicine man, and would serve as first should anything befall Kivuk.

When Anuk passed away unexpectedly fifteen seasons later, it was apparent that due to his sheer size, power and volition, Yaku would be first medicine man. No one in Point Hope rejoiced; all preferred the amiable Kivuk's medicine over the malevolent, menacing Yaku.

Eight years later and now fully matured, Yaku's immense build had become almost freakish in contrast to the size of the others in the village. Dark skin and coal black hair were the only features he shared with them. The Tareumuits were mostly a flat-faced, pug-nosed people with protruding chins. They were short in stature and had a calm, untroubled manner.

Yaku, being Athabascan Indian, had a more streamlined head and face with two deep fissures knifing down each cheek, reaching the jaw line. Thick brows roofed his dark eyes, unfeeling orbs that seldom moved. If Yaku wanted to see left or right he slowly turned his head while looking forward ardently with great concentration. He stood over six feet tall, close to seven when wearing his headdress.

Any of the men in villages across the Arctic would covet what Yaku had, but he was not satisfied. No, Yaku was anxious, desirous. A tension was building inside him. He had endured many, many days without killing. Yaku yearned for the absolute power that would come with the death of the nursemaid Kivuk. Without Kivuk's constant opposition he would be free to impose his will on the villagers.

Yaku wrestled with his hunger for many days, unable to come to a resolution. He knew killing Kivuk could bring about his end if the village elders of Point Hope and the neighboring communities of Kiana, Point Lay and Kivalena banded together against him, fearing that he would become too powerful. Would they dare?

He sought the counsel of his deity in the sweathouse and received it. The time had come, time... to gamble.

Once the winter sun had finished paralleling the horizon, Yaku commanded privacy from everyone, instructing his wives to keep his skin bag full of water and leave him be. He would stay in isolation performing a ritual in the sweathouse. They understood, all too well.

That done, Yaku set upon the task of calling his kikituk to be born. The kikituk had been dormant inside him over a year now—making a difficult labor even more strenuous. But the pain would be worth it. He began chanting, sweating and fasting. It would take days. But worth it ... yes ... worth it.

Five days later, late at night, Yaku birthed his kikituk into a pool of blood and sweat. It had four short legs, an elongated body and pointed ears. Its mouth overflowed with fine sharp teeth. The kikituk's black body was shining with afterbirth and stood eight inches from the ground to its back. Its hollow, dark, red eyes gazed up to Yaku. Although there was no need, he instructed the kikituk to Kivuk's tent and asked for his death while praising the kikituk's skillfulness. The kikituk turned and scurried from Yaku's sweathouse noiselessly into the dark ice fog. Kivuk was as good as dead.

Yaku collapsed from exhaustion, but before allowing sleep to take him, he envisioned the future. With Kivuk dead, Yaku would kill Kivuk's small sons with his walrus club as though they were baby seals, lest they seek revenge in seasons to come. The infant daughter would be buried alive with his rival's first wife. This old custom was normally no longer observed, but it appealed to him. Kivuk's other wife he would keep. Yaku fell into numb sleep with a rare smile on his face, and dreamed of himself as a powerful and ruthless ruler of many villages. His new power steeped through him.

After a time, Yaku awoke from his dreams. It was still dark out. The little demon had returned. Its eyes were glowing slightly now, a symbol of its success. Yaku became alert quickly, even though exhaustion threatened to ravage him. Yaku praised the kikituk greatly. He then began to coax the little beast into allowing Yaku to eat him so the kikituk could be kept safely inside him until needed again. The ritual was now complete. Yaku returned to near-comatose sleep.

Word of Kivuk's death spread through the village like a flock of startled ptarmigan long before Yaku woke. Messengers were sent to the other village leaders. They told of Kivuk's murder while sleeping, his throat savagely chewed away. Everyone knew who was responsible and the viciousness with which it was done. They could not stand for this, could they?

The five elders went to the tent of the ancient one to counsel. While inside, the entire village gathered around to await their decision, hemmed in murmur.

They must drive Yaku out, but how? Surely with Kivuk gone they were at Yaku's mercy, and he had none. Who would he murder next? No, this cannot remain. Yaku was too evil, too greedy. He must be driven out or the elders would all soon perish at his hands.

The elders emerged from the tent one by one, with the ancient one coming out last.

The ancient one spoke slowly in a low tone, "My brothers, we have not the power to kill Yaku. He is too strong, and without Kivuk we are too weak. But we must drive this evil from our village." He looked sternly out to his people to determine their degree of resolve. He decided to continue.

"We can do it now, while he's recovering his Kikituk, if we all band together."

The somber people looked to each other with apprehension, to the ancient one, and then nodded gravely. They knew this was dangerous, and they knew it had to be done.

The ancient one turned to allow one of the elders to speak, "Toyuk, harness two dog teams. Sitka, go with him. Takbuk, Toluk, get what you can of Yaku's furs, meat and belongings on the sleds, along with Yaku's first family." The elder reached for a whaling harpoon. "The rest of you that will, come with me to the sweathouse."

Yaku awoke to the grumbling movement of the approaching villagers. In the distance dogs barked, a baby cried. His head hurt and his body ached, but he gathered himself up, put on his bird skin parka and prepared to meet with his new subjects.

What he saw surprised him when he emerged from the sweathouse. He had not expected them to be armed for a fight. Yaku expected submission from these lemmings, not aggression. What had they left to fight for?

But theirs were the eyes of conviction, he now saw. He considered making himself larger to frighten them. But his strength was not with him yet and sensing their determination to fight, he feared he would not win.

The ancient one and the five elders stared into Yaku with resolve. He looked back at them angrily, nostrils flaring, eyes wide and irritated.

Takbuk and Toluk mushed up quietly in the two sleds with his supplies and furs in one, his two children in the basket of the other. Yaku knew it was over without a word being spoken. Still glaring, he took the sled with the furs from Takbuk. Everyone backed away slightly, eyes averted. It was quiet now but for the breeze rustling through parka hoods. His first wife was pushed through the crowd and got on the runners of the sled behind the children.

Yaku pulled the brake from the snow. Before urging the dogs on, he turned to the elders, cursed them ferociously and screamed, "Your children will suffer for this! I will return! I

4

will take the seals and whales from the ocean! The caribou from the land! The salmon from the river! Beavers from the ponds!" He paused for breath and for effect. "I will take children from their mother's stomachs! I curse you! I curse you now and from the grave!"

The women gasped, placing their hands over their mouths in horror. The men looked away, trying to hide the fear that had embraced them to their very souls.

Yaku commanded the dog team to begin. As the dogs began to pull, his wife asked, "But where will we go?"

He answered her sternly, "We will go towards the sun and stop only where there is no snow."

Yaku knew of Athabascan tribes far to the south on a beautiful peninsula of trees and mountains. Perhaps they would need a medicine man. With the dog sled moving, he turned back for a last look at Point Hope. A huge smoke plume arose from a familiar site. They were burning his dwelling.

CHAPTER TWO

Annie Moss looked up from the breakfast dishes she was washing to see the side long horizontal dust tornado indicating a vehicle coming down their road. After squinting her eyes to see farther, Annie remembered that today was the day Smokey Joe Widdecomb was coming to witch out the spot for their water well. She wasn't sure how she felt about dowsing, but everyone she had asked had told her "better safe than sorry." Besides, what could it hurt? They were just going to walk out and pick a spot anyway. Might as well have someone who thinks he knows where the water is do it, right?

But it wasn't Smokey Joe. She saw that it was Jim Bruno's tool truck. Annie put away the dish towel, leaned a hip against the counter, and watched the dirty pickup finish its approach.

Annie was surprisingly attractive for an Alaskan woman living at the end of a road out in the woods with no plumbing. She had hard elbows and bitten down fingernails of someone accustomed to chopping wood. But with her long thin frame and smooth, soft face she could put on an evening gown and fit in at any social affair. Her maple straight auburn hair was thick and seemed to be darker underneath as it moved to expose different depths, which complimented her brown eyes and thick brows. Her long cheeks burdened a kind, sometimes preoccupied smile, the corners of which turned downwards even when she cracked into a grin. She radiated the confidence and self-assuredness of someone content with her life.

The brakes squeaked to announce they had successfully stopped the wheels of the truck, and the rattle trap of shovels, tools, and loose parts of the vehicle itself gradually tapered off and fell silent.

The occupants waited briefly for the dust cloud to pass, then got out. With Big Jim Bruno was his helper Ed Tyson.

Ed was much thinner than his boss and standing together they resembled Laurel and Hardy, but with their matching coveralls they appeared professional enough, and everyone in the Homer/Anchor Point area knew they did the best work.

Anchor Point — "the most westerly highway point in North America," so identified by the huge rock marking a monument to itself. There were other highways west of Anchor Point but none that connected to the North American road system. The town spread to both sides of the Anchor River, with restaurants and tackle shops along its banks. The river flowed to Cook Inlet, meeting the big king and silver salmon that toiled to make it upstream, past nature and man, to spawn.

Sixteen miles southeast was Homer, a town of 5,000 situated beautifully on Kachemak Bay, summertime home to whales, otters, and tourists. The bay resembled a grand lake surrounded by Swiss Alps in some respects, glistening water encircled by evergreens. Huge mountains jutted up powerfully across the bay, their peaks frosted white year-round. Flowing yet still, five glaciers filled canyons from the ice field above with an aquamarine hue. On the opposite, north side of the bay, Homer spread over the bluffs and hills that faced south. Nearly every home and business, even the ball fields, enjoyed a spectacular view of Kachemak Bay and the Homer Spit. The spit was a narrow piece of land that extended five miles out into the bay. At its conclusion for all to see was the Homer small boat harbor, three canneries, a boardwalk of shops and restaurants, and a multitude of charter operations.

Both towns were located two hundred miles south of Anchorage on the Kenai Peninsula in south central Alaska. The peninsula's rugged southern coastline bordered the Gulf of Alaska, and on the west side, the side Homer and Anchor Point were on, was Cook Inlet.

With the floor beneath her creaking and talking to her, Annie moved around the kitchen counter, slid the wooden latch inside the huge door of the cabin and opened it to greet them before they knocked.

"Hello, Annie." Jim nodded toward his helper, "This is Ed. He'll be doing most of the drilling on your well."

As Annie shook Ed's hand, she observed that the good-looking blond man appeared a little ill at ease. An odd mixture of tall, yet shy, timid; perhaps he wasn't used to dealing directly with the customers.

"Sam will be here in a minute. I'm sure he saw you guys come in. He's out cutting firewood," Annie informed them while waving her hand north to indicate Sam's general location. "Would you like some coffee? I've got some lowbush muffins ready if you'd like."

"That'd be great. Thanks," Jim answered. She cooks! he thought to himself. Looking Ed's direction he saw by the sparkle in Ed's eye he'd done well to accept Annie's offer. It would also be a good idea to establish even some small rapport with Annie since up to now he had mainly spoken with Sam about drilling the well, and wives usually had questions to ask that the husbands were too embarrassed to bring up.

The two men ducked slightly to prevent hitting their heads as they passed through the huge, bear-proof door. It had to be five inches thick, constructed from two sets of dark stained rough-cut two-by-sixes, running vertically on each side of a thick plywood core. It was hung from two immense black steel hinges. A peg extending out both sides was the latch handle, which slid a thick wooden bolt into the jamb with a loud clank.

Once inside, Jim saw that the logs had been painstakingly sanded and oiled, giving them a brighter gleam than the outer sides had. The room smelled of wood smoke and muffins. Immediately to the right of the entrance was the kitchen. A large, obviously homemade wood stove was at its center with pots and pans hanging in semicircle above it. A wisp of steam escaped the big water kettle on its top, heating either for dishwater or to help keep humidity up, wood heat being so very dry. Separating the kitchen from the living room was a ceramic tile counter with stools along the entrance side. The tiles, unusual for a cabin, were a rich bronze color with splash boards extending up to the birch cupboard bottoms, accenting the logs nicely.

Annie's kitchen counter was an assemblage of semi-organized clutter. Kleenex, fruit, vitamins, mail, cookbooks and copper cans that were labeled for flour, salt and sugar lined the closest side of the counter along with wire hanging baskets imprisoning potatoes, onions and ripening avocados. On the opposite side of the sink were a rack of clean dishes and cans overflowing with spatulas, wooden spoons, ladles and other utensils. The window over the sink provided a great view of the spruce trees out front and the road leading to their driveway.

Across from the kitchen was the living room. Some second-hand easy chairs book-ended each side of a couch. The couch itself was hidden by an afghan. Part of the afghan was covered by a huge long-haired cat, whose head pointed at them with eyes closed. The indifferent mouser was named after the month Sam and Annie had purchased their boat, June. Against the wall was the showpiece of the room, a beautiful walnut gun cabinet with a glass door that allowed the rifles and shotguns inside to be inspected for quality and proper care.

Jim surprised Annie by recognizing the mellow acoustics of Earl Klugh which she had playing softly on the stereo.

Annie motioned them to the stools and pulled down coffee cups from the cupboard. As she poured, Annie looked at Jim Bruno and it struck her she had never had anyone so large in the cabin.

As Jim sat, Annie hoped the squeaking stool would hold his considerable weight. He was a huge man; all of 6' 3" or 4" and probably well over 225 pounds. She thought to herself, probably a good thing, since he wrestles the earth to give up water for a living. Jim had a small waist in relation to his barrel-sized chest. It gave Annie an impression of strength being held in check by a businessman's mind. Despite his size, Jim didn't seem at all clumsy, ungainly or bullish; his movements were fluid and deliberately at ease. An athlete in high school, no doubt. Probably had a wall full of accolades at home. He had high cheeks on each side of a pleasant smile. Neither very handsome nor homely, by far Jim's best feature was his big lake-blue eyes. His brown hair was usually covered by a ball cap, as it was today, that advertised Granite Pumps.

Unlike Ed, Jim radiated confidence and charm, sometimes a little too much, but usually his big blue eyes and beaming smile would put any apprehensive customer at ease.

Giving the initial estimate and taking in the first visual inspection of the future job site, Jim would always find something nice to say to the potential customer about their place, no matter how much of a dump it might be. It always seemed to score.

This time however, it was not difficult to find something to compliment. Sam had a nice little cabin on a good piece of land with a fantastic view of Stariski Creek and the Caribou Hills beyond. The creek snaked slowly, barely moving, through the huge muskeg expanse. The curves and bends of the water's path nearly touched themselves. Around the swamp's perimeter was a thick forest of spruce that rolled over miles of moose country. Sam had a beautiful wife who could actually cook. The muffins were outstanding; Ed was reaching for his second.

Jim, a touch envious, said, "This is a great place you folks have. How many acres?"

"Twenty, but four or five of it is muskeg directly down below where we hope the well will be, above the old caves," she answered modestly.

"I've heard about the old Thompson caves. Have you ever found any arrowheads or anything?"

Annie shook her head, "No, they're really just a couple of indentations at the bottom of the bluff. The realtor who sold us the place from old man Thompson's estate said they were Indian-Eskimo caves, but we didn't really believe her. Not until later, when we learned that before he died, Mr. Thompson let the community college conduct an archaeological dig out here."

"They find anything?"

"Not really. Some pottery fragments they glued together for exhibit at the Pratt Museum is all."

"Huh. Bugs bad out here?" Jim asked, sounding a little too interested.

Annie lifted up her shoulder, tilted her head to one side and said "Mosquitoes aren't bad, but the no-see-ums are terrible from September 'til freeze-up."

She hoped Jim and Ed couldn't sense how nervous and worried this undertaking had gotten her. If no water was found, they still were obligated to pay for a dry hole, rare but not unheard of. That was why Smokey Joe Widdecomb was always greeted with such great anticipation. The entire project hinged on his highly regarded opinion.

Jim nodded, "Yeah, it seems those little things are all teeth too."

She leaned across the counter with a Sophia Loren sideways glance, offering warm-ups. Ed, who hadn't said a word yet, mumbled a "Yes. Thank you," as he slid his cup forward.

As Annie gave the pot back to Mr. Coffee, she looked quickly out the kitchen window. "Looks like Smokey Joe comin'."

"Good." Jim had just about run out of small talk but he felt he'd done well to let Annie get to know her well drillers a bit better.

It was Smokey Joe Widdecomb all right. The car was unmistakably, distinctly Joe's, a pale, faded baby-shit green, boxy Plymouth four-door with a quarter-inch thick layer of dust halfway up on all sides. This car would have been really ugly if someone with utterly no prestige had been driving it. But with Smokey Joe at the wheel on his way to your place, it was a thing of beauty and relief once he arrived.

The car listed considerably to the driver's side. Joe pulled up and parked alongside Jim's work truck. The Plymouth rocked momentarily after stopping in a small dust cloud, proving the shocks had given out many miles ago. The driver's door opened with a reluctant creak and Joe turned and swung out one leg at a time. His wife, who was sitting next to him in the passenger seat, made no move to get out. Joe placed a hand on each side of the door frame, began to pull himself up, and after considerable effort was standing.

Jim greeted Joe, walked past him and opened the rear door of the funky car. He leaned down and retrieved some brass rods about two feet long from the floor behind the front seat while saying hello to Joe's wife. Ed moved toward the tool truck, reached over the bed and came back up with a short-handled sledgehammer and some wooden stakes painted red on the blunt end.

Sam appeared out of the trees, carrying a chain saw. He was wearing glasses and earmuffs. After setting everything down, he greeted everyone as Big Jim did the introductions, leaving out Marie. Joe's wife was ignoring them all, reading a book and chain smoking in the car.

Shaking Smokey Joe's coarse hand, Annie felt her excitement level kick up a notch. She had never seen a witcher at work before; she didn't know what to expect.

The first things she noticed about Joe were his big fat cheeks and Santa Claus belly. His white hair was crew-cut, making his ears stick out a bit oddly and accenting his beardless Santa Claus appearance in a country-bumpkin way. His cheeks held up soft, sparkling, jovial eyes that let you know he was ready to tell a tale or two. He had a fleshy chin that gobblered to his chest. Smokey Joe was dressed for comfort, not compliments. He had on very faded light-blue jean bib overalls and a T-shirt, his ensemble finished off with rubber break-up boots.

"Whereabouts would 'cho folks like me to try first?" Joe had a slow, comfortable, slightly scratchy voice that had a reassuring tone.

Sam pointed to a clearing down the hill a short distance from the cabin. "Right down toward the top of the bluff, Joe."

And with that the group began walking toward where Sam and Annie hoped Joe would find water. Joe's wife stayed in the car. Taking baby steps so as not to leave Joe behind, Sam walked alongside Joe asking questions, followed by Ed with the stakes, Annie and driller Jim bringing up the rear. In the spruce trees above, a magpie squawked to announce their entrance.

Jim and Ed didn't get paid specifically for being here now, but Jim considered it part of the total job price. Besides, even though Smokey Joe knew better, Jim needed to be here now to soothe the customer if needed and ensure the spot he witched was accessible enough to get the drill rig in and not directly under a power line or other obstacle.

Annie nodded toward the rods Jim was carrying. "How do those work? I thought dowsers used a willow branch for this."

"Some do," Jim replied. "I've seen 'em use willows, alders, crowbars, even pliers. But out of all of them, Joe here's the only one that can really do it though, and heaven help anyone who doubts him."

"But how?"

"Well you see this bend here at the end?" Jim pointed at the 90° bend that was close to six inches long at the end of each rod. "He holds on to them there, walks with this long part pointed away from him and when they cross, that's it."

Jim couldn't tell by her expression what she thought of this witchin' explanation. Annie had dropped her jaw without opening her mouth and was nodding. He had been through this routine hundreds of times and he still enjoyed watching the customers react to Joe's performance.

Even the skeptics were in awe of Smokey Joe and would hire him just to be on the safe side. After all, his thirty-five dollar fee was cheap at twice the price considering the cost for drilling the well was twenty-five dollars per foot. Jim particularly enjoyed it when those same cynics would question Joe's ability to find water. Joe would puff up, raise his voice authoritatively and bellow his customary "Mah grandaddy learnt me witchin' when ah was twelve years old! Ah'm now seventy-two years old! An' ah ain't never witched a duster yet!" Then he would go on and scold them with a story of someone local who had not witched their well first, drilled two or more dry holes, then called Joe out. He had them move where he witched and of course they hit water at a surprisingly shallow depth. Soon the doubters would almost be apologizing. Big Jim loved it every time.

Joe always strove to exude confidence and all-knowingness when he witched. Jim wasn't sure how much of this was an act, but, along with the stories Joe told, the homeowners were always won over.

When asked about the source of his amazing ability, Joe offered a vague explanation that within his body there was contained the necessary electricity needed and at that point he'd offer the rods, usually to the customer's wife, to see if they, too, had the necessary electricity. Sometimes giving them both rods, more often having them hold one while he held the other. He would then hold their free hand with his and the rods would usually cross. Whether it failed to work for them or not, the explanation of "body electricity" would suffice.

Sam directed Joe to the general area below the house where they wanted the well, and where hopefully Joe would find something. Jim came up and handed Joe the rods. Joe separated them, dangled one in each hand with his arms at his side and exhaled air out of his cheeks loudly. After a concentrated pause he lifted his hands to his chest, so the rods were level and pointing straight out in parallel, then began walking slowly.

Sam went to his wife's side and with an arm hooked around her waist, held her tightly. They looked nervously at each other and then trained their eyes on Smokey Joe, still walking slowly forward.

Soon Joe's pace slowed and he spoke, "Ah, ... ah think ahs comin' up on sumpin." He no sooner said that and the rods crossed in his hands, quickly turning inward to lay across his chest tips pointing opposite directions now. Joe stood unmoving while Ed stepped in, crouched down at Joe's feet and drove one of the stakes into the ground. Ed looked to Joe who nodded approvingly. Joe then lowered his arms, shook them like a swimmer before a race, and walked ahead about twenty steps and turned back around. Facing them now, he lifted the rods again. Since he was now walking toward them, they all could see the look of stern concentration on his face as he stared down at his rods. He walked toward them seemingly without paying heed where he placed his feet. Five feet shy of the stake that Ed had pounded in, the rods crossed again and Joe looked in Ed's direction. He was already on his way with another stake. Everyone watched Ed pound in the second stake. Sam beamed. Annie appeared delighted.

Jim knew this was his cue to move in and explain that the stakes indicated the sides of the "underground stream" and that they could follow it to get a better spot or zero in on the center where they'd already determined the edges.

But Smokey Joe continued to stand at the second stake immobile, holding the crossed rods tightly, with a staring, absent sort of look on his face.

Jim asked lightheartedly "Whatsamatta, Joe? You okay?"

Joe acted as though he didn't hear him. Instead of answering he continued to stare blankly, locked up.

Jim moved closer, put his hand on Joe's shoulder and said quietly, "Something wrong, Joe?"

Joe was startled by Jim's touch. He blinked, jolted himself awake and while recovering blurted, "Huh?... oh... yeah... fine," then spoke the routine phrase, "Dey's wadda deya."

Grateful to have Joe back with them again, Jim said, "Is it a good strong pull, Joe?" He tried to sound like he hadn't asked that question hundreds of times before.

Smokey Joe still seemed hesitant and disoriented. Jim hoped Sam and Annie hadn't picked up on Joe's preoccupation.

Pointing to a spot between the two stakes with one of the rods, Joe said, "If ya drill deya, you should have plenty of good wadda."

Big Jim looked toward Sam, hopefully without conveying the apprehension he felt. Sam nodded the final approval and Ed drove a stake, then pulled the other two. We got a spot, Jim thought to himself. At this point we'll just forget about tracing the "underground stream" since something is definitely bothering Joe.

Instead he'd go with the old stand-by, "Can you tell how deep it is, Joe?" He knew what the answer would be.

"Naw, but dey's wadda deya!"

"Okay Joe. Good deal, thanks for coming." Jim said as he pulled out and gave Joe the thirty-five dollars cash that he always paid him. He would add it to the Moss's invoice when the time came.

"No problem, Jimbo." Joe seemed relieved to be heading back to the car. "You know you can call me anytime."

Jim nodded, Yes I know, he thought, but what the hell was that all about?

CHAPTER THREE

Yaku and his family had traveled many, many days south. They were despondent now, desperate to stop, melancholy with homesickness. Yaku's wife begged to stop and start a new home. Her children were crying, sick of the confinement of the sled basket. Three dogs in the team had died and more were sickly. Their food stores were used up.

The shaman stopped, set the brake to his sled in the snow. His wife's sled came to stop bedside him. Yaku stepped calmly over to her and hit her hard. Not because she had done anything wrong, but because he must rebuild his power. Start over. The children were silent now, looking at him.

Yaku ordered them on; he would know when they reached their new home. He had sought counsel with his deity every night of the journey, and he would know it. It would be soon. He would know, soon....

CHAPTER FOUR

Pound-Growl.... Pound-Growl....
Sam was used to the feeling of disorientation that
a person wakes up with in a strange place. He'd
done it plenty, but this unbalanced feeling he awoke to now
was from a sound. A strange and never-heard-before sound
invading his ears as he opened his eyes.

Pound-Growl.... Pound-Growl....

It was actually reverberating through his bed. The pound
part of the sound was booming, the growl slow and long.

Normally, to wake up, Sam would force his eyes to stay
open and hold them open until, within a couple of minutes,
his mind and the rest of his body would follow. However, with
this booming sound, that wasn't necessary today. He was instantly awake and panic was getting a foothold on him.

Pound-Growl.... Pound-Growl....

His wife stirred next to him and mumbled, "Is that Jim
already?"

Oh, of course! Jim and Ed were supposed to start today,
early this afternoon. Sam looked over to the alarm clock and
smiled to himself when he saw it was only seven o'clock. Good
deal!

He tossed the covers over onto his wife, burying her, and
stiffly made his way over to the upstairs dormer that faced
southeast and stood there bare-assed to have a look.

There, eighty feet down from the house where Smokey
Joe had witched, Big Jim Bruno and his well-drilling rig stood
on the bluff almost directly above the old Indian caves. The cab
of the unit was a late-model GMC yellow with a white panel
across the middle where a sign proclaimed "Anchor Point Drilling." The derrick was also yellow and raised up from the back.
In fact, it was pretty much all yellow except for the cable, engine, and big gears at the rig's center. Ed was moving from
place to place, moving tools and gas cans and such. Big Jim
stood at the back of the rig, feet spread, both hands guiding a
very long stem of steel four inches or so around and, Sam
guessed, at least twenty feet long. As it was dropped and picked
up, dropped and picked up, it clicked in Sam's brain that the

pound-growl that awakened him was the rig's action. The stem being dropped was the pound and the rig gears working to lift it for another stroke was the growl sound. The derrick was impressively tall, certainly the tallest thing ever to be on his property.

He looked back at his wife in bed, eyes closed but obviously no longer asleep. He cherished looking at her when she was like this—the determination and strong will not shining through as per usual, just her cherubic beauty, vulnerable only to him. He bent down to dispatch a kiss on a turned-down corner of her mouth he loved so much. "I'll make the coffee," he whispered. She simply hummed approval back to him.

After slipping on sweat pants he took another look out the window and realized Annie and he had officially crossed a line, the line between just considering having a well drilled and being fully committed to the project.

Sam and Annie Moss had been waiting several years since purchasing the Old Thompson Place and had hauled thousands of five-gallon buckets of water home from town before they'd finally had a good enough fishing year to be able to afford having a well drilled.

Sam, now thirty-two, was embarrassed at not having water in the house for Annie sooner, but something more pressing had always seem to come up every time they nearly had the money saved. The couple had been putting off having children until the cabin was plumbed.

Baby-faced and unable to grow the standard fisherman's beard that nearly all respectable gill-netters wore, Sam always gave others a mistaken first impression that he seemed too young to be married to Annie or too young to have his own boat. At 6' 1", medium build and wiry, Sam Moss had the calloused hands of someone who made his living from the cold rough waters of Alaska, from Kodiak to Upper Cook Inlet. Sam never worried about not being substantial enough for any task, except overcoming people's initial view of him. At a first meeting with bankers, cannery management or suppliers who foolishly suggested he may be too young to handle the responsibilities, he often had to tiredly remind them that he had been carrying the mail for the last twelve years.

His rusty-blond head of hair matched the hair on his muscled arms and chest. His chin was interrupted by a dimple that Annie habitually teased him about. He always wished the dimples were in his freckled cheeks instead. Maybe then at least he'd look a little like Robert Redford. Sam had a huge nose but it wasn't obtrusive in relation to his face. He had sympathetic hazel eyes, which he thought were his saving feature. He tried to use them to his advantage to overcome his boyish appearance by looking into someone rather than at them. Sam's father had been blessed, or cursed, with the same boyish looks and, more often than not, had opted not to struggle to overcome looking years younger than his actual age. Sam had told himself early on that things would be different for him.

Sam was as well-liked here in Anchor Pint as he had been back in his hometown of Winchester Bay on the Oregon coast. He was a natural faller and could have always worked. But Sam longed for the unknown. Something far away, foreign almost. He said good-bye and left for Alaska.

During his first days in Kodiak, deck handing on a crabber, Sam, like hundreds of guys, met Annie Sterling. Annie had been there eighteen months bartending and cooking for a small but respectable bar and grill on the waterfront. Annie had politely spurned all offers, but, for reasons neither knew, Sam asked Annie to lunch and she accepted.

While the coffee perked, Sam dressed quietly and prepared a Thermos to take out to the drillers.

It felt strange to Sam to have someone else working at his place, a kind of guilt that made him feel like maybe he should be doing the work himself. But that was silly, wasn't it? Other than a shovel, he lacked the proper equipment and knowledge to drill a well. Not to mention the know-how of what to do when water is encountered. Like, what do you do when an artesian is hit, a well that flows to surface?

Sam pulled down four cups, took one to Annie. She was awake and pleased. Then he slapped open the latch on the big door to go outside to the drilling operation.

Approaching close to the rig now, Sam was both visually and audibly getting the full effect of the pound-growl noise crashing outward from the rig. With every strike of the twenty-foot-plus long stem of steel, the entire truck frame rocked back, lifting the cab slightly each time. Just before the draw works of gears would growl to lift the stem for another blow, the cable suspending the stem would slacken and slap full force into the inside face of the derrick. Combined with the derrick braces rattling, it was quite a sight.

"Hit any water?" Sam yelled, meaning it as a joke, but immediately regretted saying something so inane.

Jim handed over control of the rig to Ed and stepped back so they could converse over the rig noise. He, thankfully, ignored Sam's opening remark. It was a joke he heard on the first ten feet of nearly every well they did.

"Howdy! Waddaya think?" Jim motioned toward the rig.

"It's definitely noisy, isn't it?" Sam leaned down and poured them each a cup of coffee.

"Yes, it's really a basic method. You could say primitive, in fact, beat it 'til it goes, but it's also the most reliable."

"Hey, whatever works. You should see some of the stuff on my boat!" Sam said. Feeling a kinship with this man, a fellow blue-collar worker like himself, he handed Jim a cupful of Joe. "Me an' Annie will be headed into Homer shortly. The house will be open if you need the phone, and help yourself to anything you need to borrow out of my little shop shed."

"O.K. Great. Thanks for the coffee."

Sam set the Thermos down along with Ed's cup on the pile of casing. He watched the workers for a couple of minutes then wished them luck, waved, and went back to see if Annie was up and ready to go.

She almost was. She was seated at the kitchen-sink side of the counter with both hands wrapped around her coffee cup, brown eyes peering over its rim at him. God, he loved those thick caterpillar eyebrows of hers. He stopped noticing long ago that her left eyelid didn't open as much as the other. She had on his favorite white summer dress, casual but provocative.

"You ready to go, woman?" He was unable to conceal his excitement.

She set her cup down. Outside, the squirrels chirped angrily, apparently cussing about all the noise from the drill rig.

"Yes, just finishing my list." Annie always had a list going for town runs, chores to be done, car/home repairs pending, financial tasks to be done, Christmas shopping, you name it.

Sam stoked the fire, then closed the damper on the stove. Annie, pencil pressed to her cheek, stared at the wedding photo on the wall. The two of them exchanging vows on their boat anchored off Halibut Cove, her new husband looking so handsome. Sam went outside to warm up the truck. He swelled with pride when it fired on the first crank. Even though it was only September and not that cold yet, the birch trees had turned, and the air had that sharp, refreshingly crisp but damp smell that warned of winter.

On the way to town they talked of how their new life with water would be. No more dark trips down to the outhouse in robe and slippers, flashlight in hand. Or first thing in the morning after a snowfall had blown icy snow over the path, the wind blowing your robe open. No more getting to the outhouse to find the door frozen shut behind a fresh nine-inch drift. Never again to sit down and discover the squirrels had absconded with the t.p.

Being seen going to an outhouse is much more embarrassing than being seen going into a conventional bathroom. There is only one reason a person goes into an outhouse. You don't brush your teeth or adjust makeup. You don't wash your hands and face in an outhouse.

No more showers at the damn laundromat.

Sponge baths after sex will be a thing of the past! A sponge bath just doesn't lend itself to strolling around naked afterwards. Taking a shower at home would be so divine!

Once in town, they drove out the Spit Road to the harbor, where Annie took over the wheel after Sam got out with some hand tools he needed to work on the boat.

"See you for lunch?" He smirked at her.

"Addie's Paddies?"

"Yeah. I'll meet you at one. I'll try not to get too slimy."

"How 'bout if I just bring something down?"

"'Kay!" Lunch on the *Rainbow* with his wife sounded good, and maybe... he'd better do some cleaning in the berths.

He kissed her goodbye and walked heavily down the steep ramp. In six hours at high tide the ramp would be horizontal.

Annie watched him go in the rearview mirror of the truck. She knew why his eyes twinkled when she offered to bring lunch down; that was why she suggested it. Turning to look for an opening in traffic, she accelerated and headed off to do the shopping and other errands.

CHAPTER FIVE

"**W**ant some 'puss?"

"Naw, I'm stickin' widt the herring."

"I'm tellin' ya, ya gotta have octopus to ketch 'cha big butt."

The brothers had been out in the dirty skiff drifting for halibut for two hours prior to slack tide and all they had caught so far were Irish lords and a sea cucumber.

Ezra felt a light tug as they drifted back over their usually productive hole. "Shit, I think I got anudder one!"

Arn said to him, "I swear to God I'm gonna quit bringin' ya if all we ever gonna ketch is ugly fish."

"I do seem to get the trophy lord here lately, don' I?" Ez said back to his brother.

Arn just shook his head slowly while Ez reeled up. They were fishing in 130' to 150' of water like they'd done together hundreds of times while growing up in Anchor Point. One of the few Mormon families in a largely Presbyterian community, the boys weren't as devotedly Mormon as their parents had planned for them to be. Their clean-cut nordic appearances were betrayed by their reputations, earned from Ninilchik to the bar at Land's End on the Homer Spit.

Cook Inlet was uncharacteristically calm for the end of September. Last winter's snow cap on Mt. Redoubt mirrored off the still water. Nearly all the tourists had gone home. There were only two other boats out appreciating the fantastic scene today. The only audible sounds were an occasionally soft, wet slap of seawater under the bow and the cries of several seagulls dancing with a reluctant eagle.

Ez chided his brother, "Hey Arn, know what I read in *Sports Illustrated*? Them granola crunchers down there in California spear fish dem little halibut dey gots. Know what dey callum? Hallies! Ha! You believe that shit? Hallies!

They both chuckled bombastically.

"What would they call an Irish lord? A lordie?" Arn asked. laughing again.

The pair normally limited out before the slack tide window for drifting had passed. The average for fish size ranged from thirty to seventy-five pounds. The biggest fish they'd ever pulled into the skiff tipped the scale at Cubby's Tackle Shop at 165 lbs. The record halibut caught sport fishing was 424 lbs. and they were always looking to top it.

Finally, Ezra's weight came to the surface. But rather than the usual gaping mouth and bulging eyes of an Irish lord, there was something he couldn't recognize right away.

Arn looked down over the side and began laughing up-roariously. "Oh yeah!... You got to be good to ketch rocks!" He said between chortles.

Ezra glared back at him, "If ya blab to everybody 'bout dis you're dead meat."

"Hah! Guy's got real talent folks! Rock-ketcher, hah!" Arn chided his brother one last time.

Ez grabbed a herring head, pierced the eye with the point of the J-hook, curved it back through behind the gills, leaned his hands over the side to rinse them, then sent the bait to the bottom of the inlet to try again.

They sat in silence, randomly looking up from their poles at the majesty around them, taking turns sucking on the joint and pulling off the pint of peach brandy they brought for medicinal purposes.

When Arn's pole bent over hard, he jumped as if he'd been shocked in the ass.

"You snagged?... You're snagged, ain't cha? You on a snag? You're stuck, huh?" Ezra rapid-fired the questions.

When the pole bobbed quickly three times in succession and line started tearing off the reel, they both knew.

"Shit! You got a fish! Big one, huh? Big 'un, ain't it?"

Arn was straining just to hang on and didn't answer. He didn't need to.

Ezra immediately started to reel up as fast as he could crank. Fishermen usually formulate a contingency plan for "the big one." But when something so unexpected finally happens, the plan turns into a Chinese fire drill as boredom is ripped away like a bed sheet from a naked lady sleeping.

Ezra reeled his line in quickly and stowed his pole. He tucked away food and other loose articles in an attempt to maintain a semblance of order. That mostly done, he began untangling the harpoon line, making sure the detachable tip was rigged right. They hadn't brought the gun today; it needed cleaning. Before he'd finished, the fish went on a run and they had to strain to switch seats so Arn's line wouldn't snag on the bow of the skiff.

Pulling up a large halibut is a lot like trying to reel up a thick, muscle-bound piece of plywood, and twenty-five minutes into the fight they hadn't even gotten a look at the fish and Arn was tiring.

"Com' on wimp!" Ezra teased. "Let's see 'um !"

"Too soon." Arn panted.

"Just get 'um up so we can see 'um, then loosen the drag and let him go back down, then I'll reel for awhile."

"'Kay."

Arn pulled and reeled, pulled then cranked, Ezra leaned over the side slightly, eyes frozen to the water, the gaff and still-tangled harpoon forgotten for now.

An immense blackness came into Ezra's view.

It darkened the already dark green water even more.

"Holy Shit!" Ez paused, unbelieving. "It's a fuckin' monster! 300 pounder at least! Shit!" Ezra was yelling now, a tinge of fear coming through his voice.

Arn's eyes bugged, even though he couldn't lean forward to see yet. He kept cranking, expecting the fish to run as soon as it saw the boat and spooked as they always did. Without realizing it, after a few more turns on the reel he had the fish just below the surface.

Ezra, seized by adrenaline and excited by the prospect for a huge victory, threw the current plan out the window. He grabbed up the harpoon, stood up and held it out over the halibut's head. Arn had no choice but to go along. Ezra closed one eye, took aim, waited, then thrust the harpoon fully down into the fish's head. The fish looked directly at him. It should have flailed wildly. Curious, Arn took a step forward to try and understand what had happened. It was in that same split second looking for the harpoon line, Ez saw his brother had stepped into the coil of the line he hadn't stowed yet. Ez had detached the tip through to the other side of the fish's head and now held only the pole. As Ezra began to dive for the line there was a tremendous slap, a sickening sound and water was drenching them. The fish had been playing opossum. In the same second, the balance of slack line was in the water with the remaining line forming a half-hitch around Arn's foot.

Ez went for his knife. This was happening too fast! Got to cut it, he thought.

In a blur, Arn's foot was up against the skiff rail with a loud crash! Arn's face contorted in pain and fear.

"AHAAAAA! Arn let out a horrible wail. His foot was twisted around and *he went over*.

Splash!

Then there was nothing. No Arn, no line, no fish, no harpoon, nothing to grab. Ezra just now cleared his knife from its sheath. All that was visible in the water were millions of tiny bubbles coming up where the fish dragged Arn down.

As Arn was being pulled down into numbing cold and darkness, his first emotion upon realizing he was going to die was indignation. He never imagined himself dying before old age got him. And by a fucking fish no less! Indignation gave way to resignation. Arn took in a breath of water and was humbled.

Ezra Johnson looked up from the tiny bubbles of his brother's demise and let out an inhuman shriek. A howl of absolute, unbearable grief and frustration. An ungodly bestial cry so loud, the people in one of the boats nearby reeled in to come see if their assistance was needed.

Sometime later Ez would remember crossing a line. Only his subconscious recognized the journey he now took. Crossing the line that is always there. A short, but memorable trip for those who've made it. This line is crossed involuntarily. Once over, there's little one can do but let it take you away as if you had plunged into a deep, swift, churning river.

The particular line Ez crossed was that which separates confidence, sureness and grit from grief-stricken despair and utter resignation.

CHAPTER SIX

Sam and Annie returned home from town about four o'clock with overwhelming curiosity about what progress the drillers made in their absence.

After unloading the five-gallon water buckets from the truck and before going down to the rig, Sam gathered up an armload of split beetle-kill firewood from the shed and carried it inside. The stove was still warm. He opened the damper, then the door, raked the coals together and piled the wood on. While the fire began sucking air and crackling back to life, he searched the grocery bags for the Heineken, pulling out three bottles. With a kiss, he got Annie's permission to bail out on putting away the rest of the groceries and trotted out the door, beers in hand.

"How's it coming?"

Big Jim turned from the hole in the earth he was working over to see who asked the familiar question. What he saw was a half-smiling face with pleading, hopeful eyes, waiting in cheerful anticipation.

Jim was used to seeing this look on almost every job he did, the exception being some of the "fuck-you rich" people he worked for occasionally that could afford to go deep and didn't care if they did.

Big Jim Bruno had never worked at a job he actually enjoyed until well drilling. He'd heard on TV and read from time to time about people who loved their jobs, and he'd envied them. The first time he hit water and made a producing water well as a direct result of his own labor was the first time he'd derived any pleasure from work aside from cashing a paycheck. Jim was proud to be one of only three people on the lower peninsula who could start with bare ground and make a producing water well out of it.

He liked hitting water and then searching out the customer to tell them and everyone he saw on the way home the good news. It made him feel like a doctor coming out of surgery to tell the family of the patient, "He's going to be fine. The surgery was a success (thanks to me)." Or "She's strong;

she'll pull through." The face he was seeing on Sam now must be the same face the surgeon sees when entering the waiting room after performing surgery. He thoroughly enjoyed seeing the combination of relief and excitement on the customers' faces when he was finally able to tell them they had a well. Telling Sam and Annie would be especially sweet because they were waiting to hit water before having a baby.

He smiled at his client, walked over to him, again giving Ed the controls, "Nothing yet. We're down a little over thirty feet. We went through some sand and gravel, drilling in some soft brown clay now."

"Is that good?" Sam asked perplexedly.

"It's good for us, 'cause it drills fast, but whether or not there's going to be any water in it is anybody's guess. It'd be nicer to hit water in coarse sand and gravel than clay."

Not really understanding why that would be better, but not wanting to pester his contractor too much and sound like an idiot in the process, Sam simply offered up the beers.

"Ah! Great! Thanks." Jim set them down. "We're just about to call it a day. Tomorrow we'll be moving the other rig to a job I'll be working at the next couple of days. I went to look at it today while Ed was drilling."

Sam opened his beer and they stood watching Ed disengage the drilling gear. He pulled back on one of the controls to begin the big spool of cable rolling inward, lifting the stem out of the hole. Once the bit on the bottom of the stem cleared the top of the casing, he stopped it, then guided it out and away from the well casing, lowering it very slowly while pushing it out with his left hand. He rode the brake control with his right hand, forming a "T" out of himself with his body between rig and stem. Once the bit touched down, he locked down the brake firmly with both hands, leaving the stem standing in a manner that seemed precarious to Sam.

Ed lifted the bailer much in the same manner with a different control. As the bailer swung over the well, so did Jim's thoughts. Back to the peculiar way Joe behaved when he witched this well. Did it mean they were going to have a tough time finding water? Just what the hell was that all about?

Jim learned a lot about people's nature during his tenure as a contractor. Dealing with what a customer considers is a large amount of money seemed to bring out the real person behind the front most people have in place on a day-to-day basis. If his hunch about the strange way Joe acted was right, he'd be getting to know Sam very well.

Ed was making the last run with the bailer when Annie was seen by all three strolling down the hill toward them. With the sun getting low behind her they could almost, but not quite make out the silhouette of her lithe, shapely legs through the billowing white dress. You really couldn't see anything without using your mind's eye, just a hint of her. Sam knew Jim and Ed were looking, but he didn't mind. She was beautiful, after all, and he was just glad they were here.

She leaned her shoulder into the crook of her husband's arm, pried his beer away and took a sip. "Well? Find anything good?" She asked anyone who would answer.

"Nothing yet," Sam told her.

She pursed her lips together and nodded understanding.

Ed shut down the rig engine. He bee-lined to where the beers were, slapping his gloves together. The resultant hush that had been taken for granted up until now was so palpable it felt pleasant. They ambled up to where Jim's tool truck was parked in the driveway.

They all heard it before seeing it. That clanka-rattle-trap noise that could only be their neighbor, Roy Patterson in his black, rust-ridden, bashed-up Toyota pickup he called the M.V., in honor of one of his favorite movie stars, Arnold Schwartzenegger, whose obsession with the Army's hum-vee vehicle was widely known. M.V. stood for moving violation.

He was flying. Behind him was a huge cumulus of dust verifying his speed. He didn't rein in until nearly on top of them. When he locked up the brakes the small rocks and gravel under the tires complained loudly.

The door flew open. Out he sprang. Coming toward the group his eyes were wide, his face pursed. He panted, "You hear what happened?"

CHAPTER SEVEN

The village was small, but suited him perfectly. Yaku knew without second thought this is where his deity intended their journey to end. His wife looked at him questioningly, and he nodded, much to her relief. This tiny community of cave dwellers lived in three caverns at the base of a hill. Two small caves on the right, a much larger one to the left, evidently the chief's residence. Out across the muskeg was a creek, and in a clearing above the caves were fish-drying structures. All three caves enjoyed mostly southern exposure. A few of the women were tanning moose hides.

Yaku forcefully beckoned his dogs to stop with a sharp command and at the same time threw the brake into the coarse, melting snow. Both sleds and dogs had taken a beating in the recently deteriorating mushing conditions.

A fat man with a chief's headdress led four younger men through a door made of black bear skin covering the entrance to the largest cave. The other villagers nearby watched intently.

Yaku understood just enough of their dialect, and with a few hand gestures, was able to communicate to the chief that he was a medicine man from far away who could serve them well with his great powers. The chief hesitated, then warily bid Yaku and his family to enter his cave to eat and rest. The chief dismissed the younger men to resume their previous duties.

Early that evening, when the little community was still and gathered around the large cook fire, an anguished cry from the chief's wife was heard by all in the tribe. Anxiously they moved their worried eyes to the chief's cave. Yaku emerged and walked slowly over to the center of them. Hanging from one hand, held by the matted bloody hair, was the head of their beloved chief. Blood, gore and what must have been chunks of salmon the chief had been eating dripped from the severed neck of the horrible decapitated face, coagulating the snow beneath it into a gruesome thick red mass. Yaku's other hand held a stained hunting knife.

The women covered the children's eyes and looked away, weeping. The men stared open mouthed, immobile. Eyes wide, one of them turned away and vomited.

Yaku raised the knife slowly, threateningly.

"I, Yaku, am your leader now!" He screamed at them, knowing that though they may not understand his words precisely, they would know their meaning. In as deep a voice as he could muster, nostrils flaring, eyes wild, he yelled again, "Who will choose to oppose me?" In exclamation he threw the head onto the fire, where it began to hiss and sizzle sickeningly.

The men collectively bowed their heads in defeated obedience.

Spineless, thought Yaku. This was too easy. Could he build an army with these weakling thralls? Yes, he could. Start with the closest, small villages. Then conquer the next, and the next.

Smiling, he thought of the pleasure it would bring him to march back into Point Hope with his thrall army. They would beg for mercy; none would be forthcoming.

He stared at his new subjects a moment longer, then wiped the blood off his knife on his parka sleeve and returned to the chief's cave. Chief Yaku. He dragged the fat body of the old chief out by its heels without restraining his disgust. A background of whimpering emitting from inside the cave — the dead chief's wife, grieving.

Once he cleared the entrance, he pointed to the two largest men. "Take away this gut pile!" he bellowed, sweeping his arm to be sure they understood. The men did as they were told. Yaku could not contain his pleasure. He grinned his way back into the cave. He would learn more about these meek people from his new second wife. During the other things he had planned for her, he would learn.

CHAPTER EIGHT

After explaining to everyone about Arn's demise, Roy-Boy accepted Annie's offer to stay for dinner. Since he had brought with him such late-breaking news, Roy didn't insist on the usual arm twisting his bachelor's ego required before accepting the invitation. Roy Patterson had a house across the highway from them in the homestead adjacent to theirs. The Mosses' had the only home on any of the lots in the now-subdivided Thompson 640-acre original homestead. Roy-Boy was the Mosses' only neighbor. The remaining 620 acres were owned by a businessman in Anchor Point, J. T. Bantam, who was evidently waiting for the market to improve before developing the property and offering the lots for sale.

Roy Patterson was small in stature, hence the nickname. A mature twenty-three years old, his slim face had an elfish look. He maintained a goatee to help himself project wisdom and shrewdness, but his cordial vitality always gave him away.

He was pale even by Alaska standards. His ink-black hair and beard accented his whiteness.

"So how is Ezra doing with this, Roy?" Annie asked him from the kitchen.

"He's down at the bar, staring out into space, mumbling about that big fish's eyes. Says it looked at him, faked 'em out." Roy was perched upon his customary favorite stool. "Like that killer whale that got Richard Harris in *Orca*."

Roy-Boy had gotten a satellite dish a couple of years ago and had become an avowed movie fanatic. He now associated every situation or scenario with a movie or commercial he'd seen. His scripted existence waffled back and forth from real life to film screen life, sometimes to the point of irritation. But he was a good neighbor, always helping Annie if something came up or broke that she couldn't handle when Sam was away fishing.

"You mean like the fish did it on purpose?" Sam asked.
"Yeah."

Sam's skin chilled for a second at the thought of being pulled under. He had gaffed a lot of halibut long-lining before getting his salmon-fishing permit.

"Hey, Sammy."

"Yes?" Sam was twisting the corkscrew into the bottle of wine for dinner. On the stereo, Eric Clapton sang, then one night it came to an end, he met that girl and the trouble began.

"Do you, like, believe in reincarnation? Or going to heaven? Or Allah, or what? I mean, how could we all have had past lives if there's a couple hundred million more of us now than there was. It's not mathematically possible, is it?"

"You trying to convince me, or you?" Sam said. Looking to Annie, he saw a sparkle in her eyes that wasn't there a moment ago.

"I dunno. Arn dying's got me wondering about some things, I guess. You ever feel sometimes that the nice things about living in a small town are also the drawbacks?" Roy was full of questions tonight.

"For example?" Sam asked.

"Well, in the big city tragedy is so removed, so apart, so distant from you personally that it doesn't affect you emotionally unless it's an exceptionally heinous crime.

"But, in a small town like Anchor Point where we all know each other, the security of that is very assuring until someone gets cancer or dies in a car crash. You know them. It hits you close to home every time, and I feel guilty 'cause I kinda think maybe they died so I wouldn't have to."

"Yes, I feel that way too, Roy, but at least when you die here, there's an impact. You're more than just an obit in the back of the newspaper," Sam said softly.

Sam and Annie enjoyed the heady philosophical conversations they had over dinner with Roy-Boy. It provided them a nice break in the day-to-day drudgery, so they didn't mind that he usually showed up to visit them conveniently at dinnertime.

Sam continued, "But it would be nice once in awhile to go out to dinner, just you and the missus, without having to greet or talk business or whatever with everybody in the place. A little anonymity is nice sometimes. Then again, it sure is fine to see a friendly face if you go in the ditch or break down on the way home." He shrugged his shoulders indecisively.

A spot on the back of the wood stove was glowing now, the fire going full bore inside. Sam closed the front draft and top damper down. The stove tinked and pinged, cooling down in thank you.

"Shit, I'm startin' to sound like I'm right out of *Terms Of Endearment* or *On Golden Pond*, but I think life is like a circle, you know?" Roy continued, "You start out bedridden, an incoherent slobbering person that craps his drawers and is too out of it to walk or talk, then you end up in the same shape. But who knows what is outside the circle? I mean, before you're born and after you die?"

Sam tilted his head back and said, "I think life is about lines and what it takes to cross them. Like the lines between good and evil, love and hate, joy and grief, and the big one, life and death. But I don't know what's outside the lines though, Roy. What I'm saying is, you got me Sigmund, I don't know. You could ask the Bible-thumpers next time they knock, though." Sam smiled at his little friend.

Annie said delicately, "Arn knows."

CHAPTER NINE

The next morning Sam awoke early, excited by the prospect of getting water today. He let his wife sleep, got dressed in Carhartts, stoked the fire, and made a pot of coffee. It was too early for even the drillers to be here, so Sam headed out to the little shed that housed his tools. A sixteen by fourteen foot outbuilding across the driveway from the house on the north side of the property, it had a large overhanging roof that slanted high to low, from the front to the back, extending three feet out over the outside walls all around. In Alaska, anything that keeps the snow and weather at bay is utilized to the fullest. So the walls on the outside of the shed had tires, windows, scrap wood and metal leaning against them, sheltered by the roof's overhang. Even the upper portions of the walls were strewn with tire chains, shovels, hoes and other implements. The inside of the shed smelled of rotting wood and WD-40. A few shelves lined the interior, but the workbench and hand tools took up most of the available space.

Sam was trying to rebuild the carburetor he brought home from the boat yesterday. Not his specialty, but he had a book on Volvos he could use as a crutch to walk through it.

After an hour or so, deciding to take a break, he looked to his coffee cup. It appeared still and lifeless. Definitely cold, he thought, maybe I'll just go in and wake Annie up with an omelet.

Roy-Boy's rattle-trap came to his mind's eye when he heard it bottoming-out in the potholes of the road that led to his driveway. Roy had agreed last night to help Sam move a freezer. Sam grinned to himself when there was another louder crash from the M.V. hitting what must have been one of the larger potholes.

The rattling stopped. It sounded like Roy-Boy parked his M.V. next to the pickup. He didn't turn from the bench; Roy would know where to find him because the shed's light was on. He'd button up and put things away so they could go inside.

The door to the shed opened, closed.

"Morning, Sambo!" Roy exclaimed, a little too cheerfully for how early it was.

Sam turned to face him. Roy's left fist was clenched. "What 'cha got?" asked Sam, deliberately directing his eyes at Roy's hand.

Roy opened his hand to reveal what looked like brown flour.

"What is it?" Sam asked again.

"It's ash man, *volcanic* ash."

"Yeah? Where'd you get it?"

"From the hood of your pickup." Roy stated flatly.

"What?!"

"No shit. Check it out," he said, thumbing toward the door.

When Sam opened the door, his jaw dropped open involuntarily. The change since he'd gotten up this morning was remarkable. It was darker now than even on the cloudiest of days. The beautiful frosted yard he had crossed earlier was now an opaque gray-brown. On his face he felt sand coming down out of the sky. But it was ash, wasn't it? Looking up, it stung his eyes. There was one-half inch of the stuff covering the pickup. It gave him an inkling of what doomsday nuclear fallout would look like. He looked at Roy-Boy questioningly.

"St. Augustine blew its top, man! The top thousand feet's gone! Pretty wild, huh?"

Annie poked her head out the big front door, "Samuel!" Her voice contained a definite urgency to it, and she had used his full name like she did when angry.

"I know! We're comin' in!

"Roy, help me cover up some things, would you?"

"Feed me and I'm yours."

After covering the lumber, firewood, snow machines, and other miscellaneous items in the yard that Sam thought might be damaged by the ash, the two went inside to listen to the radio with Annie. According to KBBI, the Homer public radio station, all the peninsula was affected. An inch of ash had fallen on Homer and Anchor Point, more in Kenai. All flights to Anchorage were suspended. They advised everyone with respiratory problems to stay indoors and suggested severe motor damage could result from driving a car in these conditions.

"Will the boat be okay, Sam? " Annie asked, clearly worried.

"Yeah, as long as I hose it off before starting it up, it'll be fine." Sam assured her.

The phone rang.

"Hello?" Sam got it first ring.

"Sam, this is Jim. Say, have you got some plastic or a tarp you could throw over the rig? The less this stuff gets on the engine and gears, the better."

"Yeah, sure do. Me an' Roy will take care of that for you."

"Thanks, I sure appreciate it. Of course, we won't be out to drill until this stuff settles down. Hopefully it'll rain or snow soon."

"All right, Jim. Talk to you then." He hung up.

Annie was fishing for the breakfast pans, clanging them out as she found them. Sam could tell she was a little nervous, as she whipped her chin from shoulder to shoulder to keep her hair clear of her face.

Looking outside, Sam asked Roy, "What movie does this remind you of, Roy?"

For the first time Sam could ever remember, Roy-Boy couldn't think of one.

CHAPTER TEN

Yaku woke. Still tired, but rested. His re newal had begun.

He looked to locate his wife, to ensure she was up and going about her duties. Last night she had been tending to the cave to make it Yaku's own. It was her duty to ensure a meal for him as well as make sure he did not drink from the water bucket of a menstruating girl or eat any food of the land that had been mixed with foods from the sea.

She had kept the fire going while Yaku raped his new wife repeatedly, her cries going unanswered, but not unheard, by the others in her village. His children had pretended to sleep.

Now she lay shivering, whimpering, facing away from Yaku. The shaman swung a palm from the sitting position he was in to behind him landing it squarely on her rump. He smiled when she shrieked.

A glance at his wife brought the desired results. Water in a wooden cup. Wood. The only wood at Point Hope was what washed ashore and was scavenged. Here, they were surrounded by it. Wood. For spears, bows, arrows and clubs! He must command this work to be started at once!

His wife looked at the fire, then to Yaku. He ignored her. He had much to attend to. There was no time to eat. The dogs' well-being was foremost. If no other tribes in this area had teams, his power increased.

Yaku got up, stretched, grabbed his seal club and left the cave.

No crowd awaited him here. Not this time. Pride in his recent efforts swelled him. It was nectar to his veins, giving energy, like breath to a whale.

There were no women or children visible outside, but it was early. Three men had dug a new fire pit and were just about to light it with coals from one the fires of one of the other caves when Yaku's presence stopped them.

"Keep working!" Yaku ordered them

Further along the bottom of the bluff, just past the caves, were two other men tending to the dogs. Tethering them to small trees and stakes with strips of soft leather. Makeshift beds of hay and grass were being thrown down. All the animals' jaws were open, gnawing, trying to break down the fresh moose bones they'd been given.

This pleased Yaku. He turned his club over, stuck it under his waist belt.

One of the two seemed a little more in control of himself, a little more prudent and healthier, more muscular, than the others. Yaku could see by the knots he tied he was also knowledgeable.

"You!" Pointing, then by moving his cupped hand to his chest, Yaku beckoned the fit one to heel. *Daring* him to disobey.

The fit one did not even look to his co-worker; any gesture or resistance would be futile. The fit one swallowed, hung his head, and capitulated.

Yaku, using childish hand signals to embarrass the fit one even further, pointed to the bones the dogs were popping. "Is there more?"

So deep in his shame, the fit one became lost in his thoughts and did not realize it was he who was expected to answer. Though he understood the question, his mind had lapsed into a state of uncaring, of semi-shock.

The lack of fear in the fit one's eyes angered Yaku tremendously. Yaku must have respect! Yaku could conquer, even with thralls, and the only thing that was absolutely essential was that those under him fear him.

Yaku grabbed the fit one by the skins he wore, his other hand reached for the seal club, raised it above his head, and asked again. Screaming now.

"Are there more bones?"

"Talak!" The other man cried out to his friend. It brought him back.

"Yes, this way," the fit one said sedately, pointing to confirm the location.

Yaku followed them both through the trees to a clearing. It was a place the tribe honored the game they killed for subsistence. Caribou horns, deer antlers and the bones from many full-grown moose lay protected on make shift caches, designed to keep scavengers at bay.

Again Yaku was pleased! Such a find he had not expected. Like a child at his first bladder festival, Yaku indicated the widest shoulder and pelvic bones. These could be used for shields or helmets. Then he studied a moment and chose several racks of caribou antlers. He ordered the two dog nursemaids to bring them back. The other man looked to the fit one questioning, not understanding, near panic. The fit one murmured something under his breath and immediately they both were loading antlers and bones.

Following them back, Yaku knew he had found his go-between, his link to these weaklings! Probably the one they will look to now for salvation, since the demise of their chief. He will be first lieutenant of Yaku's army. He will serve, perhaps reluctantly, but he will serve. Yaku will see to the weapons making, then find out if the fit one has a family.

CHAPTER ELEVEN

Jake T. Bantam was suspiciously the richest man in Anchor Point, and of course, the least liked. Those that didn't know him knew of him. Low on scruples and high on profit, Bantam's entire personality was ulterior, not just his motives.

J. T. was avaricious.

He owned five subdivisions that he purchased from homesteaders, carved up, hired his grunt son-in-law Darrell Klepesen to put in roads, building pads and power, then J. T. sold the lots at a tidy profit. He owned the two gas stations, the liquor store, the only hotel in town and the jewel of his holdings, the Silver-King Lodge.

Also owned by J. T. Bantam was the general store and mercantile where he now sat in the office he kept there. For sale throughout the trading post was used furniture, some building materials, sporting goods, power tools, garden supplies, video rentals, a small area for pawned goods, and a really ugly painting. J. T. liked it and put it on the wall with a big price tag knowing full well no one would buy it.

Other than doing paperwork in the office, Bantam seldom worked the store himself. He had Charlie Brown for that.

J. T. Bantam always wore thick-heeled shoes to give the impression he was nearly six feet tall. Totally bald, his head resembled a stretch of beach after a good clamming tide. He often bragged about his twice-a-year vacations to Las Vegas, but even after visiting the desert his face remained ashen. He had a scar he would never explain that formed an "L" on his neck just south of his usually clenched jaw. His beady eyes always looked at you over a cigarette in a holder that was ever present in one corner of his mouth. He fashioned himself to look and act like F.D.R. but he didn't have the compassion to pull it off. Seldom smiling, his face had a drill-sergeant scowl that he used to his advantage intimidating people with whom he did business.

J. T.'s belly, usually covered by a golfing shirt, hung down past an oversized belt buckle and dress pants. In the pockets he always had lots of flashing cash and his keys—a huge set, cuffing together the keys to all his buildings and vehicles. When standing in conversation, he put his hand into the pocket and jangled them loudly.

When Jake Bantam was honorably discharged from the Army, he came to Alaska out of Houston to work for Rampart Oil, a big company that showcased a huge capital budget available for drilling wildcat wells. J. T. had worked on a seismograph crew, operating doodle-bug drill rigs, drilling shot holes looking for oil. After ten years of combing Alaska for oil, he was sent to head up the crew that came to work some seismic trails on the Kenai Peninsula. He met Mary Lou, then owner of the Silver-King Lodge, quit the seismic crew after they'd finished shooting all the lines in the area and went to work for her as a bouncer/bartender. In a year they were married. When she died unexpectedly, Jake inherited the Silver-King Lodge. Dubious as her death appeared to be, Bantam was never implicated. Since then he busted butt and built the restaurant and bar up into a well-known and talked-about establishment. He had parlayed his good fortune to a remarkably high level.

Most everyone called him "The General" or "The Mayor." J. T. allowed only his very few friends and poker buddies to call him by his middle name, Theo, short for Theophile.

J. T. had long ago faced the fact that most Anchor Pointers disliked him. He didn't care. He was one of the few locals with real money; they all kissed his ass when he was around. If he needed friends he'd buy 'em.

He was laboring over receivables when the buzzing and tapping of a fly on the window behind his desk disrupted him. Totally annoyed, he reached down into the waste basket, a five gallon oil can, to retrieve the Cabelas catalog he had tossed in earlier. Rolling it into a weapon, preparing to kill the insect, he halted. He thought that if the fly hitting the window is irritating him, it must be excruciating for the bug, unable time after time to penetrate through the pane of glass it cannot even see or comprehend. He decided better than killing it would be to let it continue bumping, thumping and, hopefully, suffering as penance for irritating him.

Swiveling around in his chair to observe, he blinked and was astonished to see the sky darkening with some kind of strange-looking brown snow. Momentarily stunned, he forgot all about the fly.

Though awe struck, he managed a yell. "Charlie! What the hell! Charlie! Get your ass in here!"

Kindly ol' Charlie Brown ran the mercantile for J. T. People wished that Charlie, rather than Bantam, owned it. Most of the locals waited until Jake's car was gone to go in and do their shopping. Charlie Brown was pudgy and soft but not too over-weight. He usually had an absent-minded grin on his face and Charlie wouldn't say "shit" even if he had a mouthful.

Working for the mayor was his paradox. He disliked his boss and his methods, but he loved running the store when J. T. was gone.

J. T. had sent Charlie out back earlier to destroy furniture they couldn't sell before taking it to the dump so that "none of them fuckin' prune pickers," as he put it, would get a chair or table without making a purchase. When Charlie came in through the back door, he had sandy-looking dust head-to-toe.

"What is that shit?" Jake demanded.

Charlie simply held out both hands, feigning ignorance. He hadn't the foggiest.

"Well, goddammit, find out." With that his boss dismissed him.

Charlie headed for the phone. It was a good thing J. T. couldn't read his mind. The bell on the front door tingled. They both looked toward it.

It was the well driller, Big Jim Bruno. Good. He would know what the hell was going on, and J. T. was naturally very interested in how the drilling was going at the Mosses' place since he owned the other 620 acres of the original Thompson homestead. Everyone knew he planned on de-veloping it soon, and information about water for the sub-division was pivotal. Realtors would be salivating upon hearing of water being hit in the area.

Originally, Jake planned on owning the entire 640 acre homestead after Old Man Thompson died, but the old man had explicitly instructed the executor of his estate not to sell to J. T., no matter what. Bantam had thrown old Thompson out of the bar in particularly humiliating fashion when he first began bartending, and Thompson never forgave him for it. By the time Bantam arranged for a third party to purchase the land and sign it over, the Mosses had snuck in undetected and bought the nicest twenty acres in the homestead.

"Pretty wild, huh?" Jim grinned broadly at them.

"Yeah, it sure is. But what the hell is it?" Jake demanded.

"Augustine blew its top big time. The top thousand feet of the mountain is gone. I guess we're in for an inch or two of this ash. That's why I'm here. I need a couple of tarps."

"Did anyone say, is there going to be a tidal wave, Jim?" Charlie asked him, worried.

"No, the radio said no tsunami was generated."

While Charlie showed Jim the tarps, J. T. asked him how he was doing at Moss's place. Jim knew he would.

"We just spudded in yesterday, so we're only down thirty-five feet."

"Anything?"

"Nope. Nice sand and gravel though, good for septic percolation."

J. T. nodded in the mutual knowledge that this was a good thing.

Charlie completed putting the tarps on Jim's tab, thanked him and wished him luck at Sam and Annie's.

"Thanks, Charlie. Before you drive home in this stuff, put some panty hose triple-folded over the mouth of your air cleaner. Might save your engine."

"I'll do that. Thanks."

"Keep me informed," Jake said, a little too sternly.

"Sure," Jim answered, nodded good-bye to Charlie and tingled the bell on his way out.

J. T. walked to the storefront window, the one with pictures of the Nodwell Doodle-bugs he operated years ago on each side. He looked out differently at the ash fallout this time. His cigarette holder was rolling back and forth in his mouth like a spruce log at the sawmill. Staring at the ash, he thought, the whole town was buzzing about what had happened to Arn yesterday; now this. Hmmm....

50

CHAPTER TWELVE

It was two days before anything moved. The town swept, shook, whisked, hosed and blew ash off itself. It snowed a little, too, a very thin covering, but it helped. Flights to Anchorage resumed, kids returned to school, businesses reopened.

Jim decided he and Ed would move the old 6 x 6 rig to the new Ninilchik location today. He called Sam to remind him they'd be late getting to his place.

They went to pick up the old rig at its most recent job at Dirty Dan's place near the rodeo grounds. Its derrick was already torn down and lying atop the carrier truck. It was ready to go. They greeted Dirty Dan only long enough to ensure his new well was still working and he was happy with it. It was; he was.

Jim hopped in. It actually started without a jump and he pulled onto the highway, followed by Ed, headed north. The truck seemed to Jim a bit stiff, but, after stopping for a quick inspection, he wrote it off, telling himself it was due to the new dusting of snow and recent drop in temperature.

Two miles later, just past the beaver dam in the creek below the Mad Russian's place, smoke began trailing out behind the rig, becoming thicker until Jim looked like a fighter pilot being shot down. Quickly, urgently looking for a pullout or a driveway to pull into, Jim saw nothing immediately ahead. He decided to continue for a short distance. Slowing down, he checked his mirror to see how far back Ed was. Shit! A little red foreign job had passed Ed and was between them, in the smoke.

Boom!

A thunderous body-shocking explosion ripped into the cab. Before the shock of the sound passed, a fireball came up from the floor, lapped against the passenger door, then returned where it came. Jim flinched spasmodically, his mind flashing on the sound a .44 magnum handgun makes when fired in closed quarters. The gear shifter whipped to the right then came left and slapped him on the outside of his right thigh.

He was too scared to be affected by pain. Though distressed, he maintained control and did not panic. After watch-

ing the shifter drop down through the floor where the transmission should've been, he thought, man, this is serious! and
what the hell?

Jim took a quick glance to see where Ed and the red car
were but he couldn't see either. Amazing. This was unbelievable. All he saw was a rolling embankment of intense, thick,
impervious black smoke of a type you'd see from a burning
tire after an Indy car hits the wall.

He tried the brakes. Nothing. The pedal stuck to the floor.
Still have steering? Yes! Okay, he'd just have to coast to a
stop. Damn good thing he wasn't going down Thrill Hill out
the North Fork right now. Damn!

The rig came to a gradual stop. The Preston girls, mother
and daughter-in-law had been coming in a southerly direction toward Jim and witnessed the explosion head-on. Once
out of their car, white-faced and wide-eyed, they greeted Jim
with a synchronized, "Are you all right?" They couldn't believe he actually was. Frightened, they went back to their
car.

The bottom of the seat under the driver's side was beginning to burn. Ed came up, took one look, and charged over to
the shoulder to scoop up handfuls of dirty snow. Jim joined
him, but it didn't help. The fire grew and was threatening to
engulf the entire seat.

It looked like the rig might burn completely down, right
in front of them. Jim stopped for a second to evaluate the
danger of the nearby gas tank blowing. When Ed went past
him with yet another handful of dirt and snow, Jim felt a
rush of affection and gratitude toward Ed, throwing himself
in harm's way for Jim's sake, while he himself hesitated.

Ed threw the dirt and headed for more. It had no effect.
The back of the seat was burning briskly now. Jim felt himself cross a line, the line from control to panic. From fight to
resignation. This rig was not insured. He'd let it lapse because they didn't use this rig much. He tried to cross back
over the line and get hold of himself.

A man and woman in an El Camino pulled alongside.
The man asked, "Do you need a fire extinguisher?"

"God, I hope so," said Jim, meaning that it might be too
late, but praying it wasn't.

He took the extinguisher hungrily from the man's hands at the car window. He pulled the pin, pointed it at the fire, and squeezed the lever.

"Just leave it at the Chevron," the man said and drove away, reluctant to stay. Jim never even got to thank him.

As the extinguisher ran out, so did the fire.

"Man, that was too close. What the hell happened?" Ed asked, stunned.

They looked under the cab of the 6 x 6 truck. Jim had to blink a couple times. He didn't believe what he was seeing. The transmission had sheared off at the bell housing and was hanging by the linkage and E-brake cable. Ed touched his arm.

"We got more," Ed said, pointing down the road behind them to where the explosion had started. It looked like a war zone; pieces of shrapnel, twisted drive lines and exhaust pipes, both mufflers, and the air-brake tank were scattered over both sides of the two hundred yards of road it took for the rig to coast to a stop. At the point where the transmission first blew, the road was burning in a five-foot circle and the fire was working its way off the shoulder.

"Shit!" Jim took another look in the cab of the rig to be sure the fire was staying out, then they each grabbed a shovel out of the pickup and jogged back to the fire, kicking pieces of wreckage off the road on the way.

"Christ, I don't believe this! " Jim was exasperated. The tar of the road was boiling within the circle of the road fire. Apparently the road fire was caused by the ignition of transmission oil, and further investigation indicated the shoulder fire seemed to have been ignited by red-hot scraps of steel. There were two separate fires. They decided to fight the ditch fire first. Due to the dry weeds under the dusting of snow, it was spreading faster. The road fire seemed to be burning down, not outward. They stomped, shoveled, kicked and patted until both fires were smothered. The ash everywhere seemed to have helped retard the ditch fire from advancing too fast or they surely would have not gotten it out without help.

They walked slowly back, Jim still telling himself this actually happened. He looked over at Ed.

"Ed, thanks for hangin' on me on this one, again. I'll stay and pick up this mess. Would you go and call Louie-Mac and see if they have a dump truck or something loose that can tow us the rest of the way to the job? If they don't, call the big tow truck at Inlet Muffler. We've got to get this wreck off the road and to the job. We need to be at Moss's in time today to get something done besides tearing the shit out of everything."

"Okay, boss," Ed replied sympathetically. He really liked working for Big Jim and hated to see this kind of crap happen to him.

Ed took off and Jim put what was left of his mufflers and drive lines on the rig. He was shaking a little now, as what could have happened to him began sinking in.

He got down on all fours with his butt in the air and got underneath the running board for a closer look.

"Just what the heck happened?" He thought aloud. There was a three-foot-long gash in the cab floor under the seat from the passenger side. He whistled. At the end of the three- to four-inch wide gash, which looked like it been made by a can opener, was a large twisted hunk of steel that had been stopped by the truck frame as it ripped through the floor. It was red hot at the time and then started the seat afire. It appeared to be half the emergency brake drum which had been at the back of the transmission. On the other side of the truck chassis was a full fifty-gallon gas tank.

Looking toward the front, he saw that four bolts, the front plate of the tranny and the pilot shaft were all that was left, still attached to the bell housing on the rear of the engine. Christ, what a mess! The transmission had actually sheared off! Why? The emergency brake had not been set. He supposed if it were, and the drum got hot enough, it might have fused, locked up and caused this. But... something didn't look right. The E-brake cables? What? Such a jumbled mess.

The resonating burping of a Jake brake brought him to his feet in time to see Louis, half owner of Louie-Mac Trucking, pull up in a big red Ford ten-yard end-dump. Shaking his head, Louis stopped and stood up over the open door. They'd been through this drill before.

"Got any brakes?" Louie asked without saying hello.

Jim shook his head, "I don't even have gears, Lou-Lou." He held his hand out in the direction of the cab for Louie to inspect the damage to the rig. The truck driver climbed down.

Louis whistled, "You really fucked it up this time, Jimbo! Damn! You okay? Can you steer this thing? That tranny gonna ride?"

"No, we'll cut the linkage and take it outta there." As he said it, Ed, who had pulled in right behind Louis, went for the torch and they all worked on the transmission, dragging it out from under the truck. Then they backed the dump truck up, chained up tight with a tire between the trucks and started the tow to Ninilchik.

Towed in, thought Jim. That'll just impress the hell out of them, won't it?

It was nearly two o'clock before the two drillers made it to Sam and Annie's. After Jim explained why they were late arriving, Sam suggested they ought to take the rest of the day off. It would be fine with him, but Jim declined, mumbling something about getting back on a horse.

By nightfall they were down sixty feet and hadn't hit anything but a hard sand and clay mix.

Sam came down to the rig, again with beers in hand. "Well?" he said grinning at his pun.

Jim ignored him for a moment and let the bailer fly down hole before answering. It arrived at the bottom of the well with a resounding, hollow clank! Instead of the hoped for splash. Jim lifted up on the bailer lever, reversing the direction of the drum on which the bailer line was spooled. In a few seconds the bailer was back at the surface, dry except for thick mud around the bottom eighteen inches. Jim positioned it over the trough, lowered it until it bottomed out in the cutting trough. The dump valve in its bottom opened as it always did when the bailer rested on it and three gallons or so of brown muck ran out.

"Nope, no well yet." Jim said, breathing out disappointment. Both he and Ed's coveralls were mud up to the thighs. "But we're thinking maybe tomorrow. The stuff that we're in now's got good color."

"Good color huh? You think maybe Joe witched us out some gold?"

They all three chuckled, but Sam was joking to try and hide his apprehension. Tomorrow they'd be down 100 feet or more and if they didn't hit anything that would just about take up what they had set aside for the well.

"You know, if we don't hit something tomorrow Annie and I will be stressing. But you go through the stress every job, don't you?"

Jim nodded, half smiling. A gentle look was crossing his face. Sam was the first customer he had worked for to realize that. He was really starting to like Sam. He got the feeling, looking at Sam's hands, that under the boyish look and high raspy voice Sam could be tough as birch bark. He'd have to give them a discount, once he got some water.

Jim rested the bailer against the rig for the night and threw a bucket upside down over the casing. "To keep the moose from shittin' down your well," he told Sam with a grin, and then looked at Ed and ran his index finger across his throat. Ed killed the motor and let out an "Ahhh...." at the quiet.

Sam thought that in a couple more days the noise would probably become annoying.

Jim explained to Sam over the beers that he would be at the Ninilchik job tomorrow. Ed would be here alone once Jim dropped him off. They finished the beers quickly and said goodbye.

Sam would go inside and fill Annie in. He'd try to explain the progress up to this point while at the same time keeping her from crossing the line from anticipation to worry about what tomorrow would bring.

Jim loved this time of day: the quiet, taking off muddy coveralls, getting into the warm comfortable pickup, considering the day's progress and how much money, if any, they'd earned. He enjoyed stopping in at the Silver-King Lodge for a beer with the boys and finding out what happened today in the rest of the town, the world, and if the Red Sox won.

Jim dropped Ed at home. Probably a good idea. Tomorrow would be a full, tough day.

Jim Bruno needed another beer and maybe a shot to go with it. He might feel better telling someone about what happened, if everyone didn't already know.

It wasn't the usual four or five regulars he expected to see at the end of the long mahogany bar that looked out over the Anchor River. Instead the place tonight was a real live fanny-bumper. Must be because the ash dust settled down, he thought. The tables were packed and the only time anyone sat at the tables was to eat, or if the bar stools were all occupied. Even then, customarily, the extra people stood. There was a sign behind the bar that read "All our customers bring happiness, some by coming, others by going." It rendered the owner's attitude quite accurately. Since J. T.'s wife had passed away he ordered Silver-King match books that on the back read "God made the Earth and rested, God made man and then rested, then God made woman, since then no one has rested." Pretty bold for Anchor Point.

Some of the post-World War II music J. T. loved so much, Glenn Miller's "Moonlight Serenade," was blaring from the jukebox.

Jim walked in between the bar and table touching shoulders in greeting and picking up snippets of conversation as he turned his body one way then the other to weave through.

"Naw... I've been in Anchorage since that happened...."

"Sometime I'd just like to find a man that doesn't always have a big wad of chew in his mouth and won't pee in the sink...."

"I'd rather have a sister in a whorehouse than work for them again...."

"That guy is going to drive me to jacking off!"

"It looked like two monkeys fucking a football! Hah! You shoulda seen it."

Disappointed that the place was so packed, he ordered a steak sandwich to go. He had a beer and a shot of Black Velvet while waiting, then went home with his dinner to an empty house. Better anyway. Big day tomorrow. Would have been nice to talk to someone about his day though.

CHAPTER THIRTEEN

Tripoli Herdon worked the late shift cocktailing at the Silver-King Lodge. She usually didn't get home until twelve or later if it were busy, and last night the place was packed until two. She lived in one of the trailers in the court a few paces up the hill from the bar. It was usually quiet enough during the week for her to sleep past ten, but on weekends, forget it. The children living in the other trailers woke her earlier. Her boss, J. T., was also her landlord, though she planned to break all her ties to him as soon as possible.

Everyone always called her Trippy, partly because in appearance she fit the bill of the stereotypic dingy, gorgeous blonde; partly because of her energetic exuberance. She rarely stood still, bounced rather than walked from place to place, and sometimes knocked things over or tripped herself in the process.

She did not bounce awake, however, usually not getting out of bed until nature's call demanded. Dropping her feet off the side of the bed to the floor, she hoped there would be an equal reaction and her torso would be pulled upright and vertical. There wasn't. So she moan-grunted herself up and shuffled her feet down the narrow trailer hallway to the bathroom, located as it is in all trailers, between the kitchen and bedroom.

At 5' 6", trim and tight-bodied, breasts symmetric to the size and shape of her rear, she always did well on tips in a town with few unattached females. Her blonde hair, parted down the middle of her scalp, formed an eave of bangs over her forehead. And with those green eyes she was arguably the best-looking woman in town. She was as out of place in Anchor Point as an outdoor swimming pool.

Even though she may have been clumsy at times, Trippy was far removed from being a dumb blonde. On a fast-pitch softball scholarship she received from Texas University she earned a bachelor's degree in drama, which she proudly carried to Hollywood after graduating. She quickly found out it really is tough to break into show business without knowing someone with real pull or getting a hugely lucky break. After one too many rejections and landing only small parts in commercials, she became disenchanted with the whole mess and decided she'd had enough.

It was about this time that Tripoli came across an *Alaska Men* magazine at the hairdresser's and was intrigued enough to correspond with a handsome petroleum engineer in Anchorage. She accepted a plane ticket from him, throwing caution to the blizzard.

Unfortunately, he turned out to be a real chauvinistic jerk. On an excursion to the Peninsula, they had yet another argument. She ordered him to stop the car, grabbed her bag and got out. To her semi-surprise, he drove off without trying to coax her back in. Jerk! She found herself in the smallest town she'd ever seen, Anchor Point.

From the other five trailers came unwanted sounds. A dog barking, a phone ringing unanswered and someone revving an engine and failing miserably to tune it. God, I need my own place, she thought. I need to find someone that could be a lover as well as a partner, but who? she pondered. She liked the conversations she'd had with Roy Patterson, but he was hardly tall, dark and handsome.

Trippy reached for her toothbrush and Pearl Drops, avoiding the mirror. She knew it wouldn't be good. When she first woke up her cheeks were puffy and she thought her pug nose looked bigger too. She planned on getting it fixed after her first big part. Oh, well.

Bent over and brushing, she turned on the tap. When she rinsed the toothpaste out, the taste almost made her puke. She spit, gagged, cleared her throat and spit again.

"Whew! What's the deal, huh?" She asked her cat, Brando, who had just peered around the door insolently. Trippy looked closer at the running water. It was cloudy, opaque. She let the stuff run over her finger then reluctantly had another taste. Salt. "What the..." she thought. The roof of this dump leaks better water than what comes out the faucets. Great. She headed for the phone. Hopefully *that* will work.

She called the restaurant office and asked for J. T. One of the bookkeepers told her that Mr. Bantam was not in just now but, yes, he was aware of the water problem. No, it was not just her water but everyone who was on the community system. Mr. Bantam was out trying to locate Jim Bruno now and, no, no one knew how long it would be until it would be fixed.

Okay, great. Trippy thought. She didn't have to be at work until four, but she needed a shower. Who could she call? The laundromat had showers, but....

Roy-Boy Patterson seemed like he might be a little kinky, but not so much as to be dangerous. It's not like he'd go into the garden section of the hardware store just to sniff the new hoses or anything like that.

"Hey, Brando! Do you think ol' Roy-Boy would like a visitor?" she asked the unperturbed cat mischievously.

CHAPTER FOURTEEN

Three days later, the barricade Yaku had ordered built was near completion. The blunt ends of newly splintered bones had been buried with the sharp points exposed. Lashed-together antlers, also points up, made a nasty-looking perimeter that would puncture the feet of any counterattacking tribe as well as prevent his new underlings from escaping. The look of the village was changing. With the defenses finalized, next they would finally begin making weapons.

Yaku envisioned the future. Smoke from many scattered campfires just beyond the perimeter would billow slowly skyward as his thrall army grew in size. They would be there for one purpose. To serve and obey him, to conquer for him. And one day they would march on Point Hope.

Using Talak, the fit one, as translator had quickened the readiness process. Yaku's thrall army would be ready sooner than he had planned. The dog team was well-rested now, soon he would scout his first conquest, with Talak's children in the basket to ensure all would be well when Yaku returned. The thought of his hold on these people produced a menacing smile where a scowl had been.

Yaku watched Talak and the others work. The fit one was quiet. And smart. Perhaps Yaku should reconsider Talak's role. No. Yaku pushed the complicating thought back. He had more pressing matters to attend to. Not only would these meek ones need to be shown how to make the weapons, they must be taught to use them as well.

That was a mistake. A big one. Talak was smart. While Talak worked he was thinking. Thinking and planning.

CHAPTER FIFTEEN

Jim began drilling at the Ninilchik site after seeing that Ed got started okay at Moss's. Initially starting the hole gave him a reproachable feeling that he sometimes felt when starting a new well, that he was in a sense raping the Earth and getting water would be the orgasm.

He considered himself more a miner than a rapist, except he mined for water instead of gold. Really, water is far more valuable than gold, though it doesn't pay as much. Right after air to breathe a guy's next need to sustain life is H_2O.

Man, do I need to get laid, he thought. Once he got his mind off sex, he continued to be bothered by the way Smokey Joe acted when he had witched the Moss's well! Maybe he should go talk to him if Ed doesn't get water today.

Before long, Bruno received word from Ed through his Ninilchik customer that J. T. Bantam had come by the Mosses' place. He'd been in a major panic, frothing at the mouth, insisting that Jim Bruno come to Anchor Point and look at the community water system, though J. T. didn't say what was wrong. When "The General" barked, he was used to seeing people jump.

What the hell, better go see what's up I suppose, Jim thought. He apologetically explained the situation to the customer and headed in to the megatropolis of Anchor Point. Wouldn't want to disappoint the mayor, now would we?

The drive in was picturesque. Waves of topped-out fireweed flowed like fields of wheat in the breeze. The big stand of cottonwoods on the bluff next to the ocean had shed their raiment of leaves and were naked, their only adornment an eagle perched on the uppermost branch.

The driller shivered driving past the black concave circle in the road where the rig had blown up. What's the road crew gonna think about that? Further on, he resisted the urge to stop in and check on Ed. If he'd gotten any water he would have said so when he left the message about the mayor coming by.

Twenty minutes later, Jim pulled up to the small wellhouse behind the school's baseball field. He saw the usual collection of work trucks parked next to it. Looks like the mayor called everybody for this one. They'd be very happy to see him. A plumber's knowledge of water wells was surprisingly limited.

Several years ago the town of Anchor Point had its one and only building boom. During that time the Alaska Department of Environmental Conservation's requirement of 200 feet or more between wells and septic systems could not be met because of the closer proximity of the new buildings. So the town applied for and received a grant from the state for a large diameter well for the entire immediate community. The grant also paid to run lines to the school, the lodge, J. T.'s trailers, the laundromat, community club, Wrong Way's gas station and ten or so private homes. An Anchorage driller underbid Jim Bruno on the initial installation, but Jim maintained it.

Big Jim stopped and opened the side tool box, digging out a crescent wrench, screwdriver and a powerful halogen light.

Stinky Pete was the first to greet him. Pete epitomized the stereotype of plumbers nationwide. He was forty-five, average height and over-average weight. Bruno wished Stinky would wear coveralls; the trademark crack of ass always showed over the top of his low-slung, dirty jeans. Pete always had a chew going, so his bottom lip appeared grossly distended. His teeth and chin were stained a crude-oil color. Whenever Jim saw his flat fleshy face crowding those undersized beady eyes he couldn't help but wonder what the woman that went to bed with him was like.

"Howdy, Buttercup! What's going on?" Jim asked him.

"Damned if we know, Jimbo. Me an' Jess been here nearly a hour an' all we kin figger out is that everything works fine 'cept'n the water tastes like shit."

Uh oh.

"Tastes like shit?"

"Yea, kinda salty like. Ask Jess. He tasted it."

Jess Jester's lanky frame came through the wellhouse doorway. Jess was the beloved town fix-it man. And he lived up to his namesake. Retired from the Army, his pension allowed him to trade his labor. Fixing a washing machine for the cost of parts plus a dozen eggs, replacing a leaky faucet for a home-cooked meal or even weather-stripping a window for a good joke he could tell later, Jess was a happily busy man.

Jester's lucky, Jim thought. His rhythm and mannerisms were similar to those of the black friends he'd had back home in Boston. Jester's forehead sloped back from his eyebrows to the beginning of his nappy hair. His mouth was rapid-firing; Jess liked to hear himself talk and he leaned back and cackled like a crow at his own jokes. Jim Bruno hoped he would be as content with life when he retired.

"Jimmy!" Jess exclaimed as if they hadn't seen each other in years. "Good deal! Take over man. This little honey is all yours," he said chuckling.

"Thanks, Jess. You're a pal." Jim smiled.

Big Jim Bruno wrinkled his forehead. "From what Stinky said, it sounds weird. This softener doesn't use any salt, does it, Jess?" The conditioner was Jester's department.

"Negative. Green sand. The pressure tanks and all the lines check out A-0 Kee-Dokey. You want we should stand-by and provide ground support?" After thirty years in the army, Jester still used the lingo and abbreviations. It was Jester who had started calling Jake Bantam "The General." It was especially poignant when Jess, who never made officer, called J. T., who was a drill sergeant, "General Bantam."

"Maybe for just a minute. So every house has salty water?"

"Ten-four. They're hauling water at the lodge, the laundromat's shut down, the school's got water coolers on the way, but everyone else is S.O.L." Jess said.

"We're gonna try hookin' up the old spring back to the lodge," Stinkey Pete said proudly. The spring was what the restaurant used years ago before the D.E.C. requirements. It was located down in the river bottom directly below the bar. The D.E.C. would shut the place down if they knew what Jake Bantam was planning.

This was indeed cause for concern. Jim thought he knew what was happening, but he didn't want to believe his own diagnosis. He moved toward the wellhouse.

"Jim, have you noticed how all this bad stuff's been happening around here since you guys started out at Moss's, the same day Arn drowned?" Stinkey asked, serious now.

"Yeah. Next day Augustine, then the 6 by 6 blew up right out from under me, now this." Jim shook his head sourly.

"Everybody's talking. They say it's got to have sumpin' to do wit dem old Indian Caves. Like they're haunted or sumpin." Stinkey Pete raised both hands and wiggled his fingers in a poor but funny imitation of a ghost, trying to spook Big Jim.

"So who said that? I never heard those caves were haunted. I think you're just trying to stir up some shit, Stinkey."

"I never heard that, no," said Jess. "But I seen them two caves from the seismic trail snow machining and they do look kinda spooky."

"Come on, gimme a break, huh? You two jokers are screwing with me. Go on over to the inn. I'll be there in a few and buy you clowns a couple a beers."

"Aw, do we have to?" Jess feigned whining and then cackled, his shoulders bouncing.

"Orders is orders," Stinkey echoed.

"Hey, Jimmy!" Jess yelled, walking to his work truck.

"Yeah?" Bruno could feel what was coming.

"You know why them Anchorage tourists is like hemorrhoids?"

Jim played the straight man. "No, why, Jess?"

"'Cause they're okay as long as they come and go, but when they stay they're a pain in the ass!"

True enough, Jim thought, laughing through his nose.

They both climbed into their respective tool trucks a little too eagerly. They made show of racing off, like a couple of spooked horses.

Big Jim returned to the pickup for pipe wrenches, then entered the wellhouse. It was a twelve by sixteen foot building sided with shiplap. It had an apexed gable metal roof. The floor inside was concrete with trawl lines left in it for better footing. The tall blue tanks and softening equipment sat off to the right. It was cool inside. The aroma of mildew, galvanized pipe and wet paint smacked Jim in the face. He knew from previous visits that in a few moments he wouldn't notice it, his sense of smell would adjust. If his hunch was right, he wouldn't be here long anyway. He set his collection of tools down next to the well on the opposite side of the room from the pressure tanks, shut off the main water supply valve, then killed the power. He disassembled the line coming out of the well just above the well seal and threaded on a hose adapter. Jim got a hose off the wall, connected it and uncoiled it through the door to outside. He reentered and threw the power switch. The five-horsepower pump hummed loudly in the distance. Water jerked through the hose. Jim went back outside to check on it.

Seeing the stream shooting out the hose, Jim knew that this was definitely a well problem. Might as well let it run. He tasted it. Yeech. Salt water.

He knew when State Parks built a campground down by the mouth of the Anchor River they had hit sea water. They let an unscrupulous driller from out of town take them down to over 300 feet. But, damn, the beach was a half-mile from here and this was about 120 feet higher elevation than that campground was. If sea water intrusion had reached this far, Anchor Point was in serious trouble.

Christ. First Arn killed by a fish, then Augustine goes off, then the rig blows up. I can't get any water at Moss's and now because of this salt water shit I'm not getting anything done. I better go see Smokey Joe, Jim mulled to himself.

Jim was not looking forward to talking to "The General." All he could suggest would be to keep pumping the well and hope it clears up. Or drill a new well. The further away the better. Great. Better go get it over with before having any beers. Man, this'll have him chompin' on that cig holder, won't it?

Since Jake Bantam's wife passed away he ate only food from the restaurant, declining his own cooking. Even though the house he lived in next to the bar was fully equipped and had an exceptional kitchen, the refrigerator seldom had more than milk and sodas inside. J. T. was a reformed alcoholic.

One of the waitresses could be seen from the bar carrying the mayor's dinner across the connecting boardwalk. Funny how out of place a waitress uniform always looks anywhere but in a restaurant. The waitress knocked, and went inside without waiting for a reply like she always did. No music played. The house was unearthly, uncomfortably still. She placed the dinner tray on the kitchen table like always, whether its recipient was there waiting or not. Tonight he was reading the paper, a beautiful view of the river valley beyond. The huge cottonwood trees letting go their leaves into the water. She knew better than to expect a thank you and, after setting the tray down, she averted her gaze from his ugly bald head at chest level to her. She turned to leave, thinking: How sad. He's got this big beautiful house on the best salmon-fishing stream in the world and he looks like a king in his castle with no subjects, no family, no friends. She left, thankfully happy for herself that she didn't have to go home to an empty, lonely house as well.

J. T. set the paper down and watched her butt all the way out the door. He lifted the cover off his food to see what was for dinner. A chicken-fried steak, mashed potatoes with gravy, peas and a wheat dinner roll, accompanied by the slice of raw onion he instructed the cook be brought with every meal. A side dish of cottage cheese with a red stain where a cherry must have been was also on the tray. Frowning, he was irritated at this. Not because he wanted to eat the cherry, but because he wanted to toss it himself.

A knock at the door irritated him further.

Big Jim Bruno was brushing and kicking drilling mud off himself when the door swung inward. J. T. motioned him in.

Bruno had been in the main house before, but following Jake Bantam down the hallway he was taken by the quiet. Their footsteps were loud in the sterile, dead house. The hallway opened into the kitchen/living room with an unsurpassed view of the Anchor River basin, alders and cottonwoods lining both sides of the river — very impressive.

J. T. held his hand toward a chair across from his, then picked up and relit the cigarette in the holder resting next to his food. Knocking the cigarette against the side of a nearby ashtray, he groaned, a kind of a stress groan he let out before or after phrases.

"Mmmmh... so what's wrong with my water'?"

Jim shifted uncomfortably in his chair. "I can't say with absolute certainty, but I think it's salt water intrusion from the beach."

Jim expected him to be surprised, but Bantam only nodded as if he had suspected the same thing. "Can you fix it?"

With his seismic drilling experience, J. T. probably already knew the answer to the question he'd just asked, but wanted to hear what Jim Bruno would have to say and Jim knew it.

"Possibly. I'd like to leave it pumping. It's draining off good right now, so it won't make a mess to do so. Then when I get a rig freed up, I'd like to set-up on it and surge it some. I'd also like to pump all the old shut-in wells nearby and see if they're affected." Jim tried to maintain eye contact but he didn't like looking at J. T.'s bald head. Why didn't the guy wear a wig?

"Hhpmph." J. T. didn't seem to be too impressed.

"You can tell the service board it'll be between five hundred and a thousand if they want me to go ahead." Even though J. T. was the community's biggest water user he couldn't authorize any work until the Anchor Point Service Board approved it.

Jake leaned back, puffed on his cigarette, continued to ignore his food and blew out the smoke. "Mmmmmh.... you know, a lot of folks are saying all this crap started happening since you started drilling atop them caves at the old Thompson place."

"Are you saying that we are responsible?" Christ, if J. T. was thinking along these lines then the whole town was gonna be on his ass.

"Look.... mmmmh... I don't know if it's the Devil, some kinda ghosts, or the bogeyman. I'm just telling you what I been hearing... mmmmmh."

"Well that's marvelous news, thank you. Let me know as soon as you can what the board decides to do," he said as strongly as he could muster. He rose to leave, thankful he didn't have to deal with this asshole on a regular basis. Shit, I think I'll definitely have a shot with that beer, maybe two. He closed the door and left Jake Bantam on the other side.

He stopped at the pay phone that hung on the short entrance hall leading to the bar. He dialed Sam Moss. When Sam answered, he put the dime in and after two dings Sam could hear him.

"Sam. Jim. How'd we do today?"

"Nothing yet. Annie took Ed home just now."

"How far down?"

"123 feet." Sam sounded depressed. Jim wondered if Sam had heard yet what people in town were saying.

"Okay. Did he say if anything was seeping in yet?"

"No, nothing."

Sorry I asked, thought Jim sadly. "All right, chin up and all that. Thanks for taking Ed home. I'll see you tomorrow." He signed off. Shit, 123 feet and no water.

Opening the bar door usually turned heads and once inside, cheers of greeting ensued. This time however, Jim could tell what the main topic of discussion was prior to his entrance. Everyone still said hello. Jim looked at the eyes. Were they the eyes of his conscience looking back at him? No, of course not. All the bad things happening were not his fault. He was just trying to get some nice folks water.

Jess Jester motioned him over to a stool he and Stinkey had been saving. "Well, what'd the grouchy ol' bastard have to say, Jimbo?" Jess asked him. The low din of conversation in the rest of the bar resumed.

Jim relaxed, threw a twenty on the bar and ordered a round of draft beer for them. "I told him what I thought it was. He's gonna get with the board."

"So what is it?" Stinkey Pete asked.

"Well, Sugarbritches, I think it's salt water intrusion."

"You mean, like, from the beach?" Pete had brown spit running down his chin.

"Yeah."

Stinkey exhaled a whistle, grabbed his new beer and downed it, evidently wishing to distance himself from the whole situation. He burped, then said, "I think I'll go home and see if the old lady wants to bump uglies with me. See you boys later." And he left.

"How 'bout you, Jess? You have something better to do too?"

"Jimmy, my man, as long as you're buyin', I'm stayin'."

And stay they did. Jim needed to blow off some steam and Jess was a good enough friend to stay and listen. After a few too many, Jim thanked Jester and drove home competently. More so than he'd expected. On the short drive down to his beach house he realized he really was getting depressed about all this. Was there something to what everyone was saying? He decided to worry about it tomorrow. Pulling into the driveway, the neighbors' dog was there to greet him. It usually was if he came home late and they had put the dog out for the night. He was a good-looking and well-behaved golden retriever named Barn. Jim liked the dog and tonight was feeling tremendous affection for him.

Jim's house was built from driftwood logs he'd collected off the beach with a borrowed skidder. Jim laid large cedar logs horizontally up to window height, then place the remaining logs vertically on each side of the windows that faced the beach, providing an unobstructed view of the surf, Cook Inlet and the impressive mountains of the Alaska Range beyond. To the left was Cape Douglas, the beginning of the Aleutian chain. The solidly built cabin had a thrown-together look. The floor plan was simple. One big room for kitchen, living and bedroom. The only separate room was the bathroom.

He invited the dog in with him and went directly to a cupboard, fetching down a brand new bag of Oreos. He ambled over to the couch, Barn in tow and sat down. He pried the package open and instead of shooing the dog away, tossed him a cookie. The dog caught it, chewed briefly, and gave a big wag of his tail in approval. Jim had a silly grin on his face now and threw another cookie, and another, giggling between each one. When the package was gone, he and Barn fell deep asleep.

CHAPTER SIXTEEN

*A*n enormous tree came up out of the ground where the well casing should have been. At the back of the rig, mud surrounded it at ground level, falling into the hole when the tree rose, then coming back up, obscenely overflowing on the ground as the tree descended. The tree was debauching the Earth rather than drilling it. An immense, dead tree with short, lifeless branches. It extended to the top of the derrick, much in the manner the drilling cable would, going through the mast head on the sheave.

A clear thought came. "How did Ed rig this up?'

To the left, two men stood by watching with interest. Both of them obese, bald-headed fat-cat Wall Street types in suits. The one with the cigar walked over to Jim and demanded, "We have to move it. Everything. We don't want the well here. We want it over there." And he pointed to an area about twenty feet off to the right.

That did it. It'd be enough to wake any driller. "Move the well" were three words guaranteed to get a reaction, and Jim's heart was thumping.

His eyes hurt and his head was pounding. He glanced toward the little radio clock — not even six yet; not even light yet. There was no way he was getting back to sleep, even if his head didn't hurt. The memory of the dream was there. The tree had been so... vile. What was it supposed to be anyway? So weird... He shook his head to jog loose from the image. But he knew he wasn't getting that dream out of his head until he got busy. He picked up the phone and dialed.

"Whuu... huh? Hello?"

"Ed! You sleepin'?"

"Well, I'm not anymore." Ed feigned anger.

"I'm coming to get you, Eddie. Buy you breakfast. You gonna be ready?"

"Yeah, be ready," he mumbled and hung up. Ed lay blinking himself awake and sat up. It was unusual for Jim Bruno to want to go to work this early. Likely the stress was getting to him. Ed swung his feet down to the floor, wiggling his toes into his slippers. It was the last time he would ever do that.

Thankfully, there were not many people in the restaurant at 6:20 a.m. Weird looks from your friends is a bad way to start the day off. After the waitress poured coffee and left with their order, Jim quizzed Ed about how the drilling was going at Moss's.

Ed told him that when bailing he was no longer getting back the water he'd been pouring in to suspend the cuttings. That meant it was percolating down through the sandstone formation as he drilled. Water would not be forthcoming right away. It also meant Ed would need more water to drill with today. Before they hit anything, they would need to find a clay layer or something similar that would hold up an aquifer. At least the sandstone drilled fairly fast.

Bruno decided Ed would put in one more day on his own at Moss's to show his determination and confidence in Ed. They were not panicked yet.

They finished their eggs and ham. Jim paid, they headed out to the tool truck. When they arrived just before dawn this morning it looked like a nice day was about to begin. Now with the sun breaking, a chill changed the day's character. It now looked like a tempest was possible. Dark thunderheads either just appeared or had already been over Cook Inlet but had remained unseen in the predawn darkness, the shadow of them covering the now wintry-looking Inlet.

Jim left the driver's window halfway down and now the interior of the Ford was cold.

Leaning forward to look up out the windshield Ed rubbed his hands. "This is weird."

Jim quickly rolled the window up and flipped the defroster switch to "Hi". A leaf came out of the air ducts with the air, skirting the windshield.

"Well, breathe out. Exhaling will probably warm us up faster than this heater will."

"Exhaling?"

"Yeah, you exhale at 98.6°."

"I fart at 120. Will that help?"

"Now you're talking miles per hour. Not Fahrenheit." Good, Jim thought. Ed was joking and in high spirits, or maybe just using humor to mask his concern. That was okay too. Ed worried as much as Jim did about getting water for the people they worked for, even though he only made ten dollars an hour. He cared. That's why the customers always ended up liking him so much; sometimes even more than they liked Jim, who worked so hard to win them over.

Once at Moss's, Jim got out to help check oil, fill the gas tank with the Jerry cans they had along and make sure Ed got started okay. Plus he wanted to see if anything seeped in overnight, unlikely as that seemed considering the material they were in now. But a few feet of seep into the well bore would be a promising development.

Sam was coming down the hill with coffee. He had been briefed about seepage by Ed late yesterday. The rig was started and Ed ceremoniously put on his gloves before sending the bailer down for a tag run. Except for Ed riding the brake, it free-fell for a half-dozen seconds. They all hoped to hear a splash; instead there was the same resounding clank! Ed and Jim looked at each other without lifting their heads. The look said "keep drilling."

Bad as the situation was, Bruno knew Ed could run the job solo today, Ed never crossed over any lines on the job. Though after hours it was a different story sometimes. Jim witnessed Ed step over the line from sensibility to abandonment a time or two, and had pulled Ed's car out of the ditch the next morning or helped him rebuild bridges he'd burned. But today Jim was showing confidence in his friend.

Sam reminded Jim that per their original agreement he and Annie could only pay cash for the first hundred feet and would have to make payments on the balance. Jim reiterated that would be fine.

"I'm going to the harbor today to work on the boat. Annie will be staying if Ed needs the phone or anything," Sam sighed.

"Thanks, Sam. Appreciate it," Jim said, noting a slight hunch in Sam's shoulders when he turned and went back up to the house.

Double-checking with Ed that he had everything, Jim left also, heading north to the Ninilchik job.

Before Sam left for Homer he checked in with Annie. She may have added to the list while he was outside. He had already put the carburetor in the pickup. A familiar sound began behind him after he closed the big door.

Pound-Growl.... Pound-Growl.

"You know, that sound was music to my ears a few days ago," Annie commented, not looking up from her list.

"Yes, I know. It's starting to annoy me, too."

Pound-Growl.... Pound-Growl.... Pound-Growl.

Sam continued, "At twenty-four dollars per foot, that's two dollars an inch, and that thing seems to go about a half-inch each time it hits. That's a dollar a pound!" He was trying to cheer her up with black humor. It wasn't working.

"That would be okay if it was hamburger, but this might all be for nothing!" she blurted, her eyes watery now.

He came around the counter and held her. She put a hand on his chest, then the other and looked up at his near-beard.

"We'll get it, Annie. Don't worry, 'kay? Joe Widdecomb witched it and he never misses. It's just deeper than we'd hoped, that's all."

She nodded imperceptibly, trying to hold it in. Annie swiped a finger under her eye. She kissed her husband, handed him today's list and, shooing him out, said, "Go on now, or you'll be late coming home. I'm all right."

He kissed her again and left, hoping to himself he was right. If he wasn't, what would they do with twenty acres and no water?

Reluctantly he grabbed the handles of two five-gallon water buckets to fill in town. He had assumed that he'd already done that for the last time.

Annie trailed him out the door.

"June! Kitty, Kitty, Kitty!" she called. "Sam, I haven't seen her for a couple days, have you?"

"No, but don't worry. Probably just freaked out by all the noise, is all."

Annie nodded bravely.

But June wasn't freaked. She was dead.

CHAPTER SEVENTEEN

En route to Ninilchik Jim tried to think of any wells deeper than 150 feet within a mile or two of Sam and Annie Moss's. He couldn't. Maybe I ought to call up old Tasker just to see if he has ever drilled any deep holes in the area, he thought, and deliberated the issue.

Fido Tasker was another water-well driller further north in Soldotna. Fido used to drill in Anchor Point and Homer. When Jim first arrived in Alaska, Fido hired him to work for Tasker's Well Company, Inc. Fido had treated Jim like one of his sons, teaching him all the intricacies of the business.

A cantankerous yet friendly old guy, he and Big Jim got along famously, drilling wells all over the peninsula for three years. Fido helped Jim get started on his own in Anchor Point, selling him a rig on the pay-when-you-can plan. With a little buttering up from Jim, Fido agreed not to drill in the Anchor Point area anymore, to prevent competing with his "little bud," Jim Bruno. Two years later, Jim bought a second rig from Fido Tasker.

Ninilchik, an even smaller town than Anchor Point, overlooked Cook Inlet and Mt. Iliamna beyond. The town's economic base was tourists from the world over, who chased the world-class salmon that ran from the inlet up Deep Creek and the Ninilchik River during May and June. Ninilchikans also had a small commercial fleet, a cannery and a school, grades K through twelve.

Jim pulled up to the phone booth in front of the general store and lumbered out of his tool truck and into the booth. He thumbed through the yellow pages until he found Fido's ad under "water well contractors."

**The Well Driller Who Always
Wears A Tin Hat Must Be Doing
Something Right
HERE'S HIS STATUS
SAME WIFE: 48 Years
3 BOYS: Danny, Jeff, Kevin
SAME BUSINESS: 42 Years
SAME LOCATION: Route 4,
Soldotna, Alaska
SAME SLOGAN: We need
your business. Our business is going in the hole.
Full equipped to Hydrofracture our wells or your existing well.
PLEASE CALL 262-5995
ANYTIME AND HELP RUN THIS BUSINESS INTO THE HOLE.
FIDO D. TASKER AND SONS
TASKER'S WELL COMPANY, INC.**

Likely he'd have to leave a message since it was after 8:30 now. Fido would be out working. He started much earlier than anyone, saying the early worm kicked the late worm's ass. Surprisingly, Fido picked up on the second ring.

"Taskers. Fido speakin." With the booming of the gravelly voice Jim's mind conjured up the image of his mentor and friend, with his bulldog jowls, round clown nose, laughing eyes and huge gray beard lapping at his chest.

"So why aren't you out going in the hole, Fido?" Jim asked him.

"Well, hey! Jimbo!" Fido instantly recognized him. "You *know* I can go in the hole from right here, too!"

Still sharp as ever, Jim thought.

"What's up, son? You calling to tell me you're finally getting hitched?" Fido tried to play matchmaker for Jim on several occasions with predictably disastrous results every time. Bruno never complained, partly out of respect for the wise old driller and partly out of the hope he would finally connect with someone he wanted to spend his life with.

"No, nothing as good as that, I'm afraid. I've got a problem that maybe you can help me with. Isn't that usually why I call? 'Cause my butt's in a sling?"

Fido Tasker had forgotten more about water wells and drilling on the peninsula than anyone would ever know.

"Yep. But that's okay. I like showing off. But hold the phone a minute, would ya, Jimmy? I got a Bible-thumper on the other line I'm gonna tangle assholes with."

The line went blank, on vacuum. Jim was grinning. He wished he'd been there to see Fido's face when he said that. Ha! He knew that for Fido Tasker to still be in his office this late, the place must be a zoo. Two minutes later Fido was back on the line.

"You there, Jimmy?"

"I'm here."

"Gawd, I hate them thumpers. You give them bastards a discount and then they take four months to pay you!" he said exasperatedly.

"Delayment of payment in the name of the Lord is God's will though, Fido." Jim teased. "And he works in mysterious ways."

"I'll take a boozer or a druggie anytime over those people."

"I'm with you, Fido. Hypocrites are the worst."

"So what's a matter wit 'cha?"

"Fido, do you remember where the old Thompson homestead is?"

"North of Anchor Point four or five miles, right?"

"Yeah, you got it. We're coming up on 150 feet out there. Been in soft sandstone that's so dry we can't keep any water in the hole. I was wondering if you had ever done any around there or knew of any deep ones close by?"

"We thumped a couple out there. One for Liebowitz and one for some hippie out by the highway... Lemme think... Yeah, I'm pretty sure they were both around sixty-footers though."

Jim knew the places he was referring to. He'd done some service work at Liebowitz's; in fact, he had gotten a copy of the well log for reference from Fido at the time. The hippie he referred to was Roy-Boy Patterson.

Jim explained everything that happened since they started the well and that if he didn't get water soon his name around Anchor Point would be mud.

"You anywhere near them old Native caves out at the end of the road?"

"Right on top of 'em, Fido." How did I not mention that? Jim wondered.

Fido changed the pitch of his voice, "Oooh... spooky."

"Yeah, we expected something at sixty or seventy feet." Jim let that hang for Fido to elaborate on.

"Jimmy, if you're in soft sandstone you know what you all gotta do."

Jim knew.

He bid Tasker thanks and good-bye, promising to come up and tell him how this one turned out.

Jim's hangover was fading. But his apprehension was increasing.

CHAPTER EIGHTEEN

Ed looked out from the rear of the drill rig to the same view Sam and Annie saw from their living room. By four o'clock in the afternoon the sun was lower than the tree tops opposite the Mosses cabin, casting an alpenglow farewell on the Stariski Valley below him. The Mosses didn't get the beautiful sunsets over Cook Inlet like Roy-Boy did, but Ed knew about the righteous sunrises because his tiny slab cabin had the same view, just down the creek a mile or so from here. Ed had been awakened more than once, semiconsciously believing something was on fire because of the neon-bright red color the interior of the cabin had become.

Once the sun hits the muskeg on a morning like that and thawed it, the unique familiar tundra smell always greeted a person at the front door saying, "You're in Alaska!"

The drilling was going down good but the water tank would be dry soon if Jim didn't show up soon with a refill as planned. Man, is this thing ever taking a lot of water, Ed thought.

He was holding the cable leading down the well to the drill stem in his hand as it whipped and jerked up, down, and around. This gave him a feel of what the bit was doing. He could also tell when water came into the well bore or the formation changed. Looking down, he noticed a crack developing in the steel "ear" he had welded to the casing to hold it up. They stopped adding casing two days ago at eighty-five feet when they started getting into the sandstone. He was now down over 185 feet going for the big two hundred. That meant ninety-five feet that the casing could possibly fall if that "ear" should break. Unlikely as that might be, they didn't need any more trouble right now, especially that kind. The customer wasn't liable to pay for a dropped casing. No, that would not be good.

Ed heaved forward on the lever that disengaged the main gear, shutting down the rig in mid-stroke. He next reached for the largest control and pulled hard, which spun the main bull line spool, raising the drill stem until it was up safely inside the casing. With ninety-five feet of open hole, the less time the tool string spent below the casing the better. An earthquake or collapse of any kind could ruin a guy's whole day.

Indifferent to the mud covering him, Ed trudged to the right side of the rig facing the house. The combination welder/generator unit was mounted between the rig engine, rig draw works and the back of the truck cab. He reached for a welding helmet and put it on, tightening the nut on the ratcheting headband. He paused. He'd gotten the strangest feeling someone was there watching. "Odd," he thought. "Maybe I'm just stressing." He pushed the rubber-encased start button to warm up the three hundred amp welder. The machine was also a twenty-five KW generator for 110 volt receptacles and two 220 volt outlets they used at remote sites and locations where power had yet to be installed.

Ed began his walk to the back of the rig where the welding leads and rod were kept. His hand grabbed the diamond plate catwalk for balance and was forcibly seized in a fiery jolt.

ZAP! Owww... ahhh. ..! Ed thought he was screaming. He wasn't. His last thought before losing consciousness was "such pain! How could anything hurt this bad? Shouldn't I pass out? What was...." *Craaaaack!* A loud arc flashed out of the hole in Ed's boot and after being thrown clear, five feet away from the drill rig, Ed Tyson, single white male, age 26, lay unconscious on the ground. The right side of his body began an intense, sustained muscle spasm.

Ed did not know he had just received a potentially fatal shock and significant chemical changes were taking place along the anatomical pathways inside his body's fuselage. The current had traveled along his nerves, blood vessels and muscle tissue, the paths of least resistance. His ionic impulses were completely disrupted and after ninety seconds of convulsions, Ed Tyson's heart stopped.

Annie was inside the house preparing a fish brine when she heard the drilling rig kick out of gear. She went across the inside of the cabin to the window facing the rig. Eyes averted to Ed outside, she bumped her hip into one of the end tables.

Sam had instructed her how to watch the drilling tools to see if they came out of the hole wet instead of muddy. That could indicate they may have hit water. But this time Ed stopped before the long stem reached the surface. This was different. Her curiosity was piqued. She watched him forcefully strut around to the middle of the rig and put a welding hat on over his ball cap. Then he stopped. He looked left then right. Is this some prewelding exercise or is he trying to remember something? she wondered.

Ed started moving again. When he started the welder it puffed gray smoke straight up, coughed and leveled off at high idle. Ah, he's just welding. She began to turn away from the window.

Her peripheral vision caught something strange about Ed's posture. She snapped her head back. Ed's legs were buckling and his arm seemed to have gotten caught or snagged on the side of the drill rig.

CRAAACK! She heard the lightning-like cracking noise and saw an arc flash burst out from under Ed's boot. He was jerked up and backwards, landing splayed out on his back.

"Oh my God!" She squeaked, fear and concern arresting her. Hand over her mouth, she ran the fifteen feet to the phone.

Shaking, it took her two tries to dial 911 correctly. While it rang, she stretched the cord and leaned enough to get a look at Ed. He was convulsing on the ground. The realization that she was here alone with Ed until help arrived overwhelmed her.

A woman's voice ended the waiting. "This is the Emergency Operator. How may I assist you?"

Trying not to sound as frantic as she really was, Annie pleaded, "I need help! Right now! An ambulance for my well driller, Ed Tyson! I think he's been shocked!"

"Yes ma'am, what is your name and where are you?" the much calmer voice asked.

"I'm Annie Moss, five miles north of Anchor Point on the old Thompson homestead, end of Peggy Street."

"All right. Good. And you have someone in shock? What caused them to go into shock, ma'am?"

"No, no! Not shock. Shocked, like with electricity, you know? He's on the ground shaking!"

"All right. Ma'am, please stay calm, stay on the line. I'm putting you on hold for a moment."

"Hold? No! Wait!" Annie yelled at a blank line. Leaning to look again she saw Ed was still. Very still.

Less than a minute passed. The operator was back. "Ma'am?"

"Yes! I'm here!"

"Ma'am, I've dispatched E.M.T.s with an ambulance from the Anchor Point Fire Hall. They can reach you much faster than the Homer Hospital's ambulance. Ma'am, do you know CPR?"

"I've taken a class, but it was a long time ago." Please God don't let him be dead, she thought.

"Fine, but first make sure the power source is disconnected. We don't want two victims. Next check for breathing. You may need to initiate CPR. Then cover the victim, keep him warm until the E.M.T.s arrive."

"But I don't know how to shut off the power!"

"Ma'am, if you are not certain it is totally safe, stay away. Help is already on the way. The hospital's been notified. I will call Homer Electric to see if they have a crew nearby."

"I... Okay. I'll see what I can do. Please hurry!" She hung up. Breathing in and biting her bottom lip, she paused for a second to think. She didn't want to get shocked yet she couldn't just sit here while Ed was lying hurt out in her yard.

She yanked an afghan from the couch then grabbed her fire-stoking mitts from their place next to the stove. The gloves would keep her from getting shocked, wouldn't they?

Annie slapped at the latch of the huge front door and bolted outside without closing it. She ran, afghan trailing like a cape. Stopping just short of the downed man, she put on the mitts and tried to determine the danger.

The welder/generator was running but the drill rig engine was not. What had shocked him?

She unfolded the afghan, preparing to cover Ed. His face looked pale, ashen. He was absolutely motionless. She couldn't kid herself. He wasn't breathing. Annie scrutinized top to bottom and wished she hadn't. Ed's work boot had exploded outward from the inseam to the toe, most of his foot with it. Smoke was still rising from the gash and his mangled foot tissue was open, exposed autopsy-style. Blood was coming slowly out of the fissure's lowest point. The gaping wound looked partially blackened, possibly cauterized by the burn. His hand was very red and looked as though it could be burned as well.

"Please God, don't let him die," She said, not hearing herself. Her mind raced irrationally as she thought, This is our fault. We're responsible for this. How long since he had stopped breathing? Two, three minutes? She had to act now. Ed lay prone five feet from the drill rig. Unless the electricity was going through the ground she should be okay touching him.

She stepped cautiously forward and knelt, slowly covering him chest to knees with the afghan, half expecting a spark to jump up at her hands. Blood pounded in her temples. Annie didn't need to check for a pulse. There wasn't one. Ed's skin was tinted bluish. She looked up from where she knelt at the rig, then discarded the mitts.

She squinted her eyes and swiped at Ed's chin awaiting the sting of an electric shock. None came. Okay, she thought, but, God, I'm scared! Annie tried to steady her breathing. With both hands now she tilted Ed's chin as she had learned at first-aid class years ago. Mouth to mouth or heart massage first? As she considered this, unintentionally the image of Sam came to her and she felt a twinge of guilt. Would he be jealous maybe? Annie! Get a grip! Of course not!

She began breathing into Ed. Blow... one, two, three... blow... one, two, three. His lips were cold. Blow... one, two, three; then she jumped over him straddling his torso and gave his chest five quick pushes. Nothing happened.

The Anchor Point Fire Department proudly consisted of a large two-vehicle shop newly built with shiny steel siding that stood apart in a town made of logs and rough cut. It was built with oil royalties that actually managed to trickle their way down through the fat cats to the working man's level.

To the right of the main shop doors, there was a man-door which provided another entrance to the small office. Past the office were a bare table and chairs. A coffee pot and its condiments lined the unpainted sheet rock wall.

The fire hall housed a thousand-gallon pump truck and an ambulance which the community owned before the hall was built. The town equipped the ambulance by holding countless garage sales, pie auctions and other fund raisers.

All the emergency medical technicians and firemen were volunteers, more than half women, housewives whose husbands were away working, either fishing or at the Prudhoe Bay oil field for weeks at a time. Along with being so-called slope widows, these women also shared the many hours of classes, study and training that were required to become an E.M.T. III. They also held the wish to do some good for their community. Unfortunately, most of the fire calls they went on were slab cabins or houses that were totally engulfed by the time the pumper arrived. Bad roads, no roads and spread-out population delayed them. The cause of the blaze almost every time was a chimney-stack fire which had gotten out of control.

The paramedic calls they responded to were mostly chest pains and automobile accidents. Night collisions with moose kept them as busy in the wintertime as the drunk drivers did. The last few days they had received numerous calls from elderly people with respiratory problems due to blowing ash from St. Augustine's eruption.

The E.M.T.s took turns manning the fire hall during the day only. Each took a six-hour shift every third day. At night, two people were designated on-call at home but all the E.M.T.s carried VHF radios on their belts and whoever was closest usually responded first, on-call or not.

Today, Ernie Cavanaugh and Donna Jansen were at the hall playing cribbage. They were close to going home when the hot phone simultaneously rang and blared throughout the building over the loudspeaker.

Ernie threw down his hand face-up and sprang up to answer.

"Fire hall. This is Ernie." He spoke into the mouthpiece, monotone. "Yes... End of Peggy Street. ..Roger."

He hung up. Donna already had her gear on and was opening the shop door in front of the ambulance.

Donna was a robust woman in her late fifties. She had a round face and full body but she was not really overweight.

Her hair was salt-and-pepper colored, her eyes clear and perceptive. She was a farm girl in Kansas when she heard about "The Great Land," and decided she wanted to see it. She came to Anchor Point to check on a job opening at the post office. The Alaskan spirit she encountered appealed to the cowgirl in her. Something akin to a couple of drunk fishermen in a rowboat trying to navigate dangerous rapids, laughing despite the obvious jeopardy. After landing the job, she never left.

Ernie grabbed rubber boots and some elbow-length rubber gloves. They jumped hurriedly into the ambulance. Ernie took the wheel. Donna looked at the gloves, then at Ernie's wrinkled face expectantly.

"Sounds like either Big Jim or Ed Tyson got shocked bad. Doc White's gonna call us on the radio from the hospital."

Donna was downcast. Big Jim Bruno drilled her well some time back. She liked him tremendously. In fact, had she just been a few years younger....

Two miles down the road, the radio speaker broke their contemplation.

"Eight-eleven, Ernie, this is base, come in please." The voice was calm.

Ernie lifted the mike from the holder on the dash and keyed it. "This is eight-one-one. Go ahead." Donna prepared to take notes.

"Ernie, this is Doctor White. We have an apparent electrocution victim down and likely in arrest. When you arrive at the scene, look for these symptoms: entrance and exit wounds, paralysis from disrupted nerve pathways, respiratory difficulties. You may have to initiate a tracheal tube if the tongue or airway are swollen. Check for fractures from falling and if the victim is conscious check for visual difficulties, restlessness, muscle tenderness and shock. Have you got all that?" Ernie looked to Donna; she nodded. "Roger that," Ernie answered Dr. Dan.

"Okay. Once you get him stabilized, start an IV of lactated rigers, administer oxygen at sixty-one per minute, monitor and EKG during transport and watch for ventricular dysrhythmias, copy?"

"Ten-four Doc, we got it."

The doctor came back. "Good luck. Radio us back when you have an E.T.A. and status report. We'll be waiting on you. Out."

Donna finished writing and looked at Ernie, who, after replacing the mike in its holder on the dash, was looking back at her somberly. They didn't speak, didn't need to. They knew this was a bad one.

Annie felt Ed's body jolt once, twice, then he coughed, hacked and began gasping for air. A rush of utter relief and happiness washed over her. She did it. He is alive now because of what she did! Wow! But like a wave on a steep beach it retreated as soon as she took another look at Ed's foot. God, where are they? she pleaded to herself. Trying to overcome her exasperation, she decided to get some scissors and peroxide for what was left of his foot.

Before going back to the cabin, she took another look at the exploded boot, hoping a better idea of what to do would come to her. Annie's emotional roller coaster took her back to the top when she thought she heard a car. Nausea was threatening to join in the ride.

Ernie and Donna pulled the ambulance up to the Mosses' cabin. The drill rig was not hard to find with the yellow derrick towering over the property. Looking toward it, they saw Annie Moss bent over a body that didn't look big enough to be Jim Bruno.

"Oh, man," Ernie said solemnly.

Annie turned around and saw it was the ambulance. The retired postmaster (Donna, wasn't it?) ran to her, carrying what looked like a big tool box. She motioned them with a wave away from the rig. The menacing welder was idling as if coiled and ready to strike once someone came within reach.

"God, am I glad to see you two," she exhaled.

"Looks like you're doing okay," Donna said nodding down at Ed while her hands opened the box. "Did you have to resuscitate him?" Ed's skin color was just beginning to come back. Donna took his pulse.

Annie described what had taken place: the flash under Ed's foot, his being thrown clear and his convulsions. She estimated his heart was stopped for two or three minutes.

Annie recognized the man with Donna. Ernie Cavanaugh. On permanent disability from the longshoremen. She would always see the rough-looking elderly man at the VFW fund raisers.

"Must've had a hole in his shoe," Ernie said, mostly to himself, as he unfolded the stretcher.

"Well, if he didn't before, he certainly does now," Donna answered. She wrote down Ed's pulse then picked out a gnarly looking pair of scissors from her box. She began cutting, while Ernie helped hold the leather out from the sock. She cut down to the sole then, with Ernie holding Ed's ankle up, slowly slipped the boot off. She hadn't adequately prepared herself to see this kind of damage. Only the upper side of the foot was intact. The entire underside was blown off, mutilated, blackened. Only a flap of heel dangled by a tendon.

Donna gagged. She battled back and dug into her box yet again.

A yellow and black utility truck with a Homer Electric emblem on the door was pulling in. Annie, having never seen a wound so severe, was grateful for an excuse to move away and went to greet them and explain the situation. Even though it was not their utility that caused the injury they agreed to help. Donning huge black rubber gloves, rubber boots and hard hats, they each pulled out 5-foot-long fiberglass poles with a control at one end and a pincher-type grabber on the other. They then walked calmly over to the foreboding drilling rig. After a brief once-over, one of the men reached his pole into the welder and shut it off, halting its monotonous threatening idle.

Ten minutes later, Ernie and Donna had Ed Tyson ready to be transported. They inflated a type of clear plastic bag around Ed's foot, suspending it from the ankle down. They bandaged his hand. Ed had an oxygen mask on and Donna carried an IV bottle that was plugged into Ed's arm while the HEA crew helped load the stretcher.

Suddenly everyone was gone except Annie. She made it inside to call Jim at his job site in Ninilchik, but once inside started trembling. The realization of what just occurred closed around her like a cinch strap.

She did not want to make this call, partly because Jim didn't need anymore grief. He'd had more than his share lately, and partly because he might say, "enough is enough" and give up on their well. She chastised herself for being so selfish. If he wanted to quit she couldn't blame him. She shakily opened a cabinet. After wiping the dust off the brandy bottle they had since Christmas, she poured a shot. Though she seldom drank anything other than a glass of wine over dinner with Sam and Roy, she downed the shot of brandy in two swigs. Still unsteady, she poured herself another. She set about the unpleasant task of calling Ninilchik to tell Jim as easily as she could that Ed left for the day, on a stretcher.

The late outgoing tide dropped the floats in the small-boat harbor below the reaches of the sun and, of course, Sam along with them. The sun struck only the mast tops now, setting four minutes earlier each day this time of year. The cooling air smelled of salt, crab and fresh halibut. It smelled only slightly salty; not what you would expect for a harbor. Alaska smells aren't always vivid, an example being the way freshly cut Christmas trees in Alaska have little or no smell.

Sam had been below deck changing out a bilge pump. The temperature drop caused him to consider calling it a day. He climbed out and stood, as he often did, looking at the spot astern where he and Annie were married.

The day had been fantastic, the boat drifting across Halibut Cove on a rare, beautifully warm Alaska summer Saturday. The preacher and a dozen close friends were on board. Other than Annie's mother, no family members had been able to afford either the time or money to make the trip. Sam had been happy as a baby tasting king salmon for the first time.

When the floating reception ended, he put all the guests ashore. The two of them went back out to spend their wedding night anchored off Yukon Island. The biggest of several islands in Kachemak Bay, Yukon was home to moose, deer, and many different species of sea birds. The island's bays provided safe anchorage. The evening breeze kicked up a four-foot chop and they had wild sex without any effort other than just trying to hold on to each other. Later Sam commented that it was probably the next best thing to sex in zero gravity, which would be the ultimate. Annie agreed.

Sam's wonderful daydream was disrupted by the white bucket overflowing with gangions and salmon hooks. It was the exact same type he had to stop and fill on his way home. The same type that grated on him when he heard the lid being pried off. The same type Annie had to pour water from into the kettle on the stove to heat water for dishes or sponge baths. God, taking a shower at home would be so great! He'd been wondering all day how the well at the house was coming along. He suddenly had a strong urge to shut down and call Annie from the pay phone at Addie's Paddies. He wanted to call but didn't. He closed up the boat and headed home. The anxiety of not knowing was getting to him, but he didn't want to call and be depressed all the way home to the cabin, either.

Jim just barely said good-bye to Annie on the phone. He hurriedly explained to the Ninilchik customer, then jogged to the pickup and began racing toward the hospital, maxed out, heedless of the speed limit. His mind was racing as fast as the truck. God damn it, he thought. He should have stayed with Ed today. How could so much shit go wrong so fast? Why had Smokey Joe acted so strangely? It was still gnawing at him the way Joe was so uncharacteristically stilted. Joe would never intentionally witch out a dry hole, would he? Of course not. Jim was determined to go see Smokey Joe tonight if Ed was okay. God, if he wasn't... Was there something to this voodoo shit everybody was talking about? The hell with that noise. Ed was hurt and Big Jim Bruno was pissed. He was steamed and thinking, I don't give a shit if it's ghosts, aliens, devils or fucking KGB mad scientists. I'm going out there and kick its ass! But how? Who could help me figure this out? Who? Yes, I've got to see Smokey Joe tonight. Maybe I should call Tasker again.

Jim's conscience chided him for speeding through Anchor Point. Luckily no one seemed to be around to disapprove. This time of the day the town was deserted. Strange... Could everyone know about Ed already?

Arriving in Homer finally, Jim cut off another motorist, and was rewarded with the finger. He turned left on Pioneer Avenue and drove up the hill leading to South Peninsula Hospital. The hospital was located on the uppermost street above

Homer. The medical facility had an unequaled view of Kachemak Bay, Grewingk Glacier, and the Kenai Mountains surrounding the Harding Ice Field. If you had to be laid up, a guy could do a lot worse. The bottom floor consisted of labs, a boiler room, cafeteria, laundry and administration. All patient rooms were upstairs along the view side of the building. Across the hall on the top floor were the X-ray, operating and birthing rooms, along with the ER, the nurses' station, and the emergency/ambulance entrance, a huge ramp on the right side of the structure.

Big Jim knew exactly where Ed would be. The admissions woman gave him a disapproving look from behind the counter. He caught the elevator to the nurses' station without speaking to her. Must have been the work clothes; he had not peeled off his coveralls yet.

Dr. Dan White and two nurses were delicately hovering over Ed. He was in the emergency room out cold. Tubes going in, tubes coming out. They had placed an oxygen mask over his nose and mouth. Ed's hand was seared. Grotesquely blackened and partially sutured, Ed's foot looked like he'd stepped under a lawn mower. This and Ed's overall pale appearance stopped Jim mid-step. He'd seen Ed too drunk to function but he had never seen him completely incapacitated. This was a real shock to Big Jim Bruno. He hadn't prepared himself for this mentally. The blonde, square-faced Dr. Dan saw his friend and came over to speak with him.

"We've got him stable, Jim," he said in a reassuring tone while moving Jim with him slowly down the hall. "Annie Moss probably saved his life. She got him breathing again before the E.M.T.s arrived, and soon enough to prevent any possible brain damage, we think."

"He wasn't breathing?" Now Jim was pale.

"No, he wasn't. Cardiac arrest is the major cause of death with victims of electrocution. Many bodily processes depend on ionic impulses, and these can be disrupted by electrical shock. The extent of damage depends on volts and amperage, site of contact, and resistance of the skin. I must tell you Jim, these effects are not always immediate. I've had patients survive shocks to the neck or head and then develop cataracts in their eyes up to three years afterward."

"That won't happen to Ed, will it?"

"No, it shouldn't. It appears the current flowed directly from his hand to his foot. What we are very worried about is damage to nerves, muscle and other tissue along the path the electricity traveled. Electrocution burns from the inside out, and significant chemical changes can take place. He's got third-degree burns over most of his hand where the current entered, and, as you saw, the exit wound is much more severe. He likely will lose his foot, but more critical is the damage to blood vessels and nerves that have less resistance to electricity that could disrupt or shut down certain bodily functions."

"What do you mean lose his foot? Are you going to cut it off?" Jim asked, incredulous.

"You saw it, Jim. There is not much left. That is not my call though. A surgeon from Anchorage is flying down now and will be here within the hour. I need to get Ed's next of kin from you, along with your worker's compensation carrier."

Jim simply nodded agreement, stunned. He was going numb.

"And the OSHA investigator will be wanting to talk to you and will probably want to go out to the site." Sensing Jim's worry, Dr. Dan lifted his eyebrows and told Jim, "He'll be okay Jim. His vitals are good. Look. He'll be able to lead a normal life with a prosthetic. Hell, Ralph Plymire's got one. I golf with him up in Soldotna. He does fine."

Jim could only nod again, trying to choke back the emotion that was about to become artesian.

Dr. Dan patted him on the shoulder. "He'll be all right, Jim. Now go to the office and give them his mother's or next of kin's phone number in case he doesn't regain consciousness before the surgeon arrives, okay? Then go home. Once we work on him, he'll be out until late tomorrow. Besides, you look like shit."

The profanity coming from an unexpected source in an attempt at levity almost worked. A half smile partially took over the stare consuming Jim's face.

"Thanks for taking care of him, Doc," Jim managed to say.

After straightening out the bitch in the admissions office, Jim walked to the pay phone and dialed the Silver-King, dime ready for when someone answered.

Jim recognized Trippy's velvety soft voice.

"Bar."

At the other end Tripoli Herndon listened to the dead air indicating someone calling from a pay phone. It was customary to wait at least a minute for the ding-ding of the dime going through before telling the caller you can't hear them and that they should try another phone.

Ding-Ding. "Hello, Trippy?"

Her heart leaped in her chest at the sound of Big Jim Bruno's voice. Why? She thought him to be kind of handsome in a big-guy way, and he had great blue eyes. He was articulate compared to most of the smelly fisherman Neanderthals that came in hitting on her, but he hardly ever looked her way.

"Hi, Jim. Sorry to hear about Ed. How is he?"

"Thanks to Annie he's alive, but he may lose his foot." Might as well tell everyone now, Jim figured.

"God, Jim, I'm sorry."

"Thanks, Trip. Is Jester around?"

"Yeah, hang on."

It was quiet when she set the phone down. No jukebox playing J. T.'s forties music, no loud clatter, just Trippy telling Jester, "Phone's for you; it's Jim" and then some murmuring by her, probably telling the bartender Ed's condition.

Jester's voice came over the line. "Hey, Jimbo, how ya' doin'?"

"Actually, Jess, I'm a little shook, but I'll be all right."

"Can I do sumpin', Jimmy?"

"That's why I'm calling, Jess. Can you meet me out at the Mosses' in the morning and help me figure out what the hell happened?"

Jess hesitated, then answered apprehensively, "Roger that, Jim. What time?"

"About eight. I'm going to Smokey Joe's tonight."

"Ten-four, see you at oh-eight hundred." Jess paused "Are ya' goin' to keep drilling, Jim? Everybody in town, least those brave enough to come out of their quarters thinks you should cease fire and retreat."

"I'll see you in the morning, Jess. And you can tell anyone that asks I said, 'Hell no' — I'm not going to stop drilling at Moss's.'"

"That's affirmative, Big Jim, will do."

Sam made it home just after dark. He parked next to the M.V. Sam hoped that since Roy-Boy was here, maybe that was a sign that the drillers hit water today. Sam kicked the ash off his shoes and opened the big door. Instead of a celebration he found Roy trying to comfort his red-eyed wife. Her swollen face told him today had not been a good day. She was biting her bottom lip.

"What happened, guys?" he said, crossing the living room toward them. Roy got up to get Sam a drink and refill his.

"Ed got shocked, shocked real bad. I...I saw it happen."

"Shocked? How?" Sam's concern and confusion showed in his voice.

"The welder shocked the hell out of him just like Odd Job got it in *Goldfinger*. Annie here saved his life," Roy-Boy said, pointing to her proudly.

Annie was sitting with one arm around an upright leg. She had her fingers interlaced with the toes of her other foot. It made it look like she had three hands.

Sam moved in to hug her. "You all right?"

"I was fine until everyone left. Then I kinda got the shakes, so I called Roy."

"I guess we don't have any water yet, huh?" He had debated bringing in the damn water buckets.

Still hugging her leg with one arm, Annie slowly turned her head from side to side, "No. Ed was down 185 feet last time I went out and took him a muffin. Then the... the um...

"Annie said Ed's foot was real bad," Roy-Boy interrupted to save Annie from going through it again. "Damn near blew it off."

Sam was holding Annie now. "Sam, what are we going to do if we don't get any water?" Annie said what they'd all three been thinking.

This was the unthinkable. Their property would devalue. They would have a decision to make about either raising kids without water or moving.

Sam breathed deeply through his nose and said, "Well, you know J. T. would buy it. He could pipe water in from a well off one of the other lots. But that is not going to happen. Jim Bruno won't give up on us."

This time for once Roy-Boy kept to himself the movie this scene was starting to remind him of.

CHAPTER NINETEEN

Yaku woke from an unusually deep sleep in absolute darkness, coughing, his throat burning painfully. His nostrils hurt, the cave was cool. Immediately he looked to the fire, he could barely see a few dwindling coals. Why did his lungs burn so? The smoke had drafted out of the chasm nicely before. But it was so stuffy now...

Yaku jerked up and looked to the cave's entrance. Nothing. Where edges of the bear hide flaps that covered the entrance should be visible, was darkness. Yaku could not even tell where the entrance was. He placed a hand next to him where his new wife lay. Gone. This was very wrong. His first wife and children were coughing awake now, too, and crying with fear.

He felt-crawled in the direction he thought the entrance to be, but hit his head on something hard much sooner than he expected. Groping with his hands, he felt logs, snow, ice and dirt. He now understood what they had done.

"Accursed thralls!" He screamed feverishly. Mistakenly thinking they could hear him, he tried to frighten them again.

"Remove this at once!" He yelled louder this time.

It hit him. This hole was now a tomb. He would not be able to dig out before the air was all used. He was like a seal without an air hole. The fire was already out from lack of air.

He screamed again. Not words this time. Just rage.

A moment later, he was feeling around the cavern floor for his seal club. When he found it, he quieted his family by clubbing them to death. He would need all the remaining air for himself in order to have time to curse this tribe and their land before he died.

Yaku was warmly wet with what he knew to be his family's blood, though he could not see. He realized he would never see anything again. He anger rose to a fever pitch.

"Bastard thralls!" he screeched.

Feeling until he found his amulet, he contemplated doing his worst to them. To wreak havoc from the grave. Yaku did not have time to birth his kikituk, but perhaps....

CHAPTER TWENTY

On the drive out East End Road to see Smokey Joe, Jim chastised himself again for not being there with Ed today. Trying to get too much done at one time, he told himself. He hadn't called ahead to Joe's but there was no need. Smokey Joe Widdecomb and Marie, his wife of fifty years, seldom, if ever, left the house after dark. Jim tried to release the misplaced anger he was feeling toward Joe. After all, Smokey Joe wasn't responsible for all that had happened, was he?

As long as Jim had known Joe, he and Marie lived just past the blind corner which was preceded by the Homestead Tavern and Liquor Store six miles east of Homer. Jim slowed for the blind corner and rounded it, seeing the sign "Smokey Joe's Old Fashioned Smokehouse" emblazoned on plywood atop Joe's mailbox. Joe gave himself the nickname "Smokey" in hopes of boosting sales of his smoked fish. The fish wasn't bad, but he was better known as a well witcher. It didn't bother him though. He made as much money from witching as he did from smoking fish.

Joe and Marie's residence was a broken-down trailer in need of paint. Entrance to the trailer was achieved by going through a large attached Quonset hut, converted into dirt-floor greenhouse, that was perpendicularly connected at the trailer's center. The condition of the place kept many of Joe's potential visitors from stopping, even though he invited everyone he witched for to "come on out ta da smokehouse!"

Strangely enough, the smokehouse was, in fact, far nicer than Joe's Quonset/trailer. It was two stories, about fifteen feet square, and built from skillfully milled rough-cut limber that had turned gray shortly following construction because it was never treated or stained.

Jim pulled in and parked. He threw his cap on the dash and wiggled his fingers through his hair, trying to flatten it somewhat. The big, wide-shouldered man ambled out, then turned sideways to pass under the "vestibule" leading to the Quonset greenhouse door. Smokey Joe had created "the veranda," as he also called it, from from alder poles and slabs.

The door creaked in pain when Jim opened it and stepped inside. It was empty and lifeless now, except for some pumpkins and dried, dead tomato stalks.

Marie, a notorious chain-smoker, opened the trailer door and greeted him with her twinkling eyes. A little too warm inside. At the door, one expected to have to brace oneself for the onslaught of noxious odors. But once inside it wasn't bad, although it didn't smell like fresh baked bread, either.

When Jim declined the coffee she offered, Marie went back to her ironing, cigarette dangling from her wrinkled lips. Jim was ready for something stronger and, being teetotalers, Joe and Marie couldn't offer anything.

Ol' Smokey Joe was leaned back in his tattered pale-green Lay-Z-Boy armchair, his attention divided between television and a crossword puzzle. He was straining the middle of his faded-blue bib overalls and T-shirt he was wearing, even though he probably hadn't gone anywhere today. Did he sleep in those overalls too? Jim wondered to himself.

"Howdy, Joe. How are you?"

"Jim..." Joe nodded his combination chin-neck in greeting.

"Joe, I guess you probably heard about us not getting any water out at Moss's place yet." Jim knew he had.

Smokey Joe was a type of town counselor for those who didn't get their therapy by bending the ear of a bored bartender. This was also how Ol' Joe kept in touch with goings-on in and around town. Those who came by for advice or information usually found themselves leaving some too, and they were traditionally rewarded to one of Joe's life stories. Joe and Marie shared an eventful life together. Even in the land of the rugged individualist, Joe stood apart. In his lifetime he had been a professional boxer, tried his hand at gold mining, worked in oil fields overseas, commercial fished in Alaska's early days and even helped build the Al-Can Highway during the war. Obviously he hadn't made a fortune at any of his occupations; his wealth was in knowledge and experience.

"How far down are ya, Jim?" Joe asked, a little apprehension showing now.

"We're coming up on 200 feet. Did you think it was gonna be that deep?" Jim said. He'd been glancing up at the inwardly rounded ceiling. When he looked back down at Joe, he seemed to be avoiding looking at Jim. Not at all his usual, open self.

"Naw, I didn't. But deys wada deya Jim, you keep going." That was what Jim anticipated Joe would say, it's what he had said on a couple of other occasions when they'd drilled further than expected without hitting any water. He decided to go ahead and ask him the next big question anyway.

"Joe, did you feel anything different when you witched that well? Anything unusual?"

"Well..." Marie stopped mid-stroke with her ironing and Joe, his mouth open, started to finish his sentence then apparently thought better of it. He looked at his wife, now ironing again, lifted his shoulders, turned his palms over and said, "No, not really, Bud. Why?"

"Because of everything that has been happening since we started drilling out there. And today, Ed was badly hurt." Jim hoped the words would sting Joe.

Marie, her wrinkled face now full of concern, said to Jim, "What happened to Ed? Is he okay?" she was fond of the soft-spoken Ed Tyson.

"He was electrocuted by the welding machine. He's in the hospital and it looks like he'll lose his foot."

"Oh my! I'm sorry, Jim." She came around from the ironing board, sat down in a worn stuffed chair, lit another ciga-rette and looked intently at her husband.

"I got a real good pull, Jim, but nuthin' else."

Disappointed, Jim rose to leave.

"Jim, are there some old Indian caves or something out there?" Marie, uncharacteristically, was doing the talking now.

"Yes, there is supposed to be. I haven't gone down over the hill to check them out, but I probably will tomorrow."

Marie kept it up. "Have you thought about talking to Professor Alton over at the community college? He should know 'bout them caves if anyone does."

Bingo! This was why he'd come. He knew something was up. The usually talkative Joe wasn't saying anything. Yet he was, through Marie. Telling him who could help.

Interesting...

Why hadn't he thought of this himself? The famous Pro-fessor Dan Alton, Homer's own authority on Native history. It was widely known that Professor Alton was one of the most prominent and sought-after lecturers on the circuit. He was requested from Ivy League schools as well as West Coast universities. His name and byline appeared frequently in the Anchorage newspapers. He also spoke on behalf of major Native associations and their shareholders at museum functions. His name was synonymous with the Institute of Native Archives in Anchorage.

Still standing, with his hand now on the doorknob, Jim apologized for coming so late. He thanked them and headed out through the dormant greenhouse.

After Jim Bruno left, Marie said to her husband, "You should have told him, Joe. You've been friends too long to keep things from each other."

"I wanted to, but he wouldn't have believed me. Besides, he'll find out soon enough." Joe glumly returned to his crossword.

Jim drove back through Homer, struggling to convince himself it wasn't too late to call on Professor Alton. His desire to do so was great, like a drunk craving that first drink of the day. It was now after ten. He could not risk alienating the one person who might be able to help. Damn!

The weight of his work backlog, the problem with the community system in Anchor Point, the mounting list of repairs that were now needed on his equipment, combined with today's events at Moss's were beginning to take their toll on Jim. He felt himself teetering along the line separating optimism from hopelessness. With Ed on the injured list, Big Jim was facing it all alone.

Replacing Ed was not an option. Jim would do what he could to help get Ed back on his foot, so to speak. Jim Bruno felt he owed it to Ed to wait for him. Not just because Ed most likely lost a foot today, but also for the year of backbreaking work Ed had given, in miserable conditions, without a single complaint. The next time he saw Ed he knew what Ed would ask him, and he wanted to be able to tell Ed Tyson that, yes, they, the two of them, got water at Moss's. Maybe that would help.

Bruno wishfully considered rinsing away his depression with a couple hours of Black Velvet before going home. Going to Moss's in the morning with a hangover would be a bad idea, however; he semi-decided against it.

He doubted this melancholy feeling would leave him any other way. He longed for someone to be waiting for him at home keeping the fire going. Someone like Annie who would share the everyday stress of life as well as the joy.

Jim recalled a solitary swan he had once seen on Wanda Lake in Prudhoe Bay. He felt a kinship with that graceful creature. Swans are always seen in pairs; they mate for life. If you saw one alone it meant its mate had perished. The remaining swan was condemned to a life of aloneness. How tragically romantic, he mused introspectively, to feel always as he did now.

When Jim tried to visualize someone compatible enough for him to connect with for life, only one person came clearly to his mind, Tripoli Herndon. Jim wanted a partner with whom he could laugh at the world. She looked great when she laughed. That was the problem, wasn't it? She was too beautiful. He had a tough time keeping his eyes off her, that is until she looked directly at him. Jim then became so self-conscious he lost his train of thought and speech and shyly looked away. Sometimes he thought he could feel her gaze afterward. Jim knew a person was supposed to make eye contact, but he'd always bail out, telling himself next time.

Bruno pulled the tool truck into the Silver-King's gravel parking lot and stopped, without getting out, leaving the motor running. He was in a space that allowed him an unobstructed view of the bar through the front window. Jess Jester was no longer in the bar. Jim recognized the three local men seated at the bar bringing glasses to their joyless mouths listlessly, indifferent as cows chewing on cud. At a window table were a man and woman he'd never seen before. Otherwise, the only other people in the place were J. T. and Tripoli.

"The General" still worked behind the bar on occasion even though he could afford not to. He did so partly to save money on wages, partly to measure receipts against nights he didn't work, partly to check for pilferage, and partly to keep up with what was happening in town.

Most of the time, other than doing the book work, Bantam would work the bar and restaurant in a different way. The way an entertainer works a room. J. T. would light that cigarette in its holder, stick his chin up, put a buck in the jukebox and play some vintage World War II songs and stride through the place like MacArthur recapturing the Philippines. The thing was, everyone, tourists and locals alike, loved it. When Bantam made the rounds, husbands appreciated someone interrupting the conversation with their wives, people who were buying (Jake always knew who) were vindicated by his honoring them, talking directly to them. When Jake Bantam stopped at the table, children settled right down. Even the non-tipping church-goers liked his stopping by their meal to share his conservative views.

Jim continued sitting in the tool truck. Two spaces over from him, Darrell Klepesen pulled in and parked his loud, rusted-out Ranchero. Thankfully, Darrell didn't notice Jim and went directly inside. Jim was relieved. Along with most Anchor Pointers, Jim didn't much care for Darrell Klepesen and certainly didn't want to chat now.

Darrell was a greasy, twenty-seven year old man, 5' 9" tall and on the heavy side of two hundred pounds. He had a pockmarked sheep-dog face and sticky black hair that covered his forehead to the top of his eyebrows. His brown eyes were darkly translucent as ice cubes floating in cola. His clothes were soiled. Unlike most locals, Darrell never elicited an enthusiastic group welcome when he entered the barroom, nor did he ever expect one. When son-in-law Darrell Klepesen went to work for J. T. performing the mayor's dirty work, he crossed a line. Everyone knew it. He crossed the line that separated integrity from selling out.

To the untrained eye it appeared Bantam hadn't seen Darrell enter, but when Darrell sat down on a stool and flipped the hair out of his eyes, a draft beer was already waiting in front of him. When you were a swamper for J. T., the first one was on the house.

"The Mayor" looked at Darrell expectantly from the other end of the bar as he made another round of fresh drinks for the couple at the table. Darrell acknowledged J. T.'s glance by touching his thumb to his index finger. J. T. only nodded in approval.

What was that all about? Jim speculated to himself in the idling tool truck.

Trippy came bouncing up to the waitress's station to pick up the drinks J. T. just made. She appealingly blocked Jim's view of Darrell Klepesen. Jim's eyes locked on her. She turned with the drinks on a tray and sashayed through the empty tables. "God, she is so saucy." Jim wished he had the guts to go in and talk to her. He envisioned the conversation:

"Hiya, Big Jim! Have you fixed my water yet?" she would ask, to which he would have to answer, "No." Then Trippy would sigh in disappointment. Not very impressive.

"Hell with it," he said to the steering wheel. Jim put the clutch in, shifted into reverse and backed out. Maybe next time.

CHAPTER TWENTY-ONE

Jim Bruno awoke without a hangover. Before making coffee or even brushing his teeth he called the hospital. He was told that, yes, Doctor White was at the hospital. Could he hold? Jim sat down at his little table that looked out a window set between two upright driftwood logs. The panorama of the beach beyond was not as enjoyable to view as it was yesterday.

A weary voice came through to Jim's ear. "This is Dan White."

"Doc, it's Jim. I'm calling to see how Ed's doing."

"Jim, we couldn't save the foot. There was just too much gone. The surgeon from Anchorage, Dr. Alexander, and myself conference called with Ed's mother last night. She gave consent. She'll arrive late today from Pittsburgh. Ed should be coming around then. Right now his vitals are good. We don't think there is any serious internal damage but we'll know more about that once he's conscious." He paused, "I'm sorry, Jim."

"Yeah, me too. Thanks for everything you've done, Doc. I appreciate it."

"It could have been much worse. It could have been his hand, and if Mrs. Moss hadn't been there...."

"Yeah, you're right. I'll see you this afternoon." He knew Dr. Dan was right but it still didn't help much.

"All right. Alexander is going to monitor him while I get a little sleep. I'll need to be there when he regains consciousness. Oh, and Jim," he paused, "the OSHA investigators were here, said they're coming to see you next."

"Okay, thanks again, Dan," Jim said, hanging up without cradling the receiver. He dialed the number of the community college in Homer. The receptionist rewarded his request by connecting him to Professor Alton's office.

"Alton," a stern Gregory Peck voice challenged.

Imagining a burly lumberjack type with a large black beard alternately puffing on a pipe and speaking into the phone, Jim began his pitch.

"Hello, professor. My name is Jim Bruno. I own Anchor Point Well Drilling. We're currently drilling a well at a site just above the old Thompson caves. Are you at all familiar with the area?" Jim partially held his breath, hoping the professor was going to help.

"Why, yes. In fact, I took a class on a dig at the base of the caves six years ago, with Mr. Thompson's permission, of course."

"Would you mind telling me the results of you findings?"

"Not at all. It was essentially a disappointment. What little we did find is on display in the Native Alaskans Exhibit at the Pratt Museum. Some pottery fragments, leather-working tools, couple of projectile points and some garment needles made from salmon bones."

"Hmmm..." Jim quickly tried to think of how he could explain the precariousness of the situation he was in without sounding like a crackpot.

"Professor, we've been experiencing some difficulties out there...I wonder if I could discuss it with you later this afternoon."

This piqued the professor's interest. His throaty voice changed in pitch and the words came closer together. "Yes, certainly. My last class is over at three thirty."

"Would four o'clock be all right then?" Jim asked.

"I'll tell the receptionist to expect you."

Jim thanked him and gradually hung up. Smokey Joe had implied this man knew something that could help. But what?

Bruno stopped at the Tesoro station in Anchor Point, loaded up on gas and filled the barrels with water for drilling. He poured coffee into his Thermos and grabbed a couple of candy bars and a sandwich to go with the grapefruit he brought for lunch. The never-to-be-completed gas station/bait store was a favorite stop of Jim's. The owner, Wrong Way Bremmicker, and Jim had been friends since Jim had first come to Anchor Point. There was always plenty of bantering between Jim and the guys who worked the pumps for Wrong Way. They were all Yankee fans. Wrong Way was from Saranac Lake and friendly bets for who bought beers were made whenever the Red Sox played the Yankees.

While the attendant filled the tool truck with gas, Jim carried his Thermos in. Wrong Way was there, stocking the cooler with the sandwiches his wife made every day.

"You going to drill on the 'well from hell' today, Jimbo?" Wrong Way asked abruptly, an edge of concern in his voice.

Jim knew whatever he told his friend would soon be known to everyone in town. All the locals who stopped for gas also came in to chat with Wrong Way and get some horrible but free coffee. The station could have been named Anchor Point Telegraph.

"Yep, I'm meeting Jester out there to try and figure out what the hell happened yesterday."

"How's Eddie doin'?"

Jim swallowed. "They had to amputate his foot. His hand is burned pretty bad. I'm going to see him this afternoon and find out more. I'll let you know."

Wrong Way nodded his head slowly while closing his eyes at the same time in quiet solemn understanding.

Bruno paid his tab total after filling the barrels with water. On his way out he said to Wrong Way, "Wish me luck, would you, Buddy?" This job gave not wanting to go to work a whole new meaning.

"You know I do, Jim. Hell, I think the whole town's waiting for you to get water out there."

Jim pulled away and rattled onto the road. With every bump, water splashed out of the barrel's bung holes like whales breaching. Wrong Way and the attendant looked at each other for a moment in silence, then went back to work.

In the distance, seventy miles to the southwest, the volcano Mount St. Augustine continued to billow smoke over Cook Inlet as if to say to the town: "Don't piss me off; I can do it again."

CHAPTER TWENTY-TWO

Percy Liebowitz was an austere man that enjoyed showing off his fitness by taking a brisk walk out his gravel road to the row of mail boxes on the highway. He had made the mile-and-a- half journey every day since retiring from teaching, regardless of weather conditions. He would pick up his mail and get the paper, returning just as rapidly as he had come. He was proud of his trim physique. He still had most of his own hair and teeth. Not bad for a man his age.

Percy accepted his life was in its twilight years. The first few months of his retirement had been spent soul-searching. In the end, he reluctantly acknowledged his own death as inevitable. He conceded only after attaching a precondition, a stipulation, to his life's term paper, that final graduation.

That his death would be as his life had been, dignified. He would go gracefully, not whining and crying like some punk on death row screaming, "I didn't do it!"

Liebowitz considered himself a civilized man in a community of barbarians. Other than his daily excursion to check the mail, he seldom left his house. He, instead, remained content to open the pages of the newest bestseller by Robert B. Parker, Ed McBain, Tom Clancy, Clive Cussler or Robert Ludlum, spy novels being his only vice. Today, Frederick Forsythe's newest effort, *The Hammer of God*, arrived from the book club.

With no one driving by on the highway for him to give a self-satisfied wave to, he began the walk back home, opening mail as he went. While reviewing this month's electric bill, something in his peripheral vision seized his attention, ordering his eyes to look directly ahead.

A large cow moose was standing in the center of the road, facing him squarely.

Percy observed moose in the wild on nearly a daily basis, considering them, as did many in Alaska, to be part of the landscape. Up to this moment he had never considered the power a moose possessed. Subconsciously, he perceived his superior intellect as something that would prevent any dumb animal from harming him or even threatening to.

He knew cow moose with calves charged people who got between the cow and their offspring, but this moose was alone. Calving season ended months ago.

So they stood there. Two pig-headed old timers, neither one about to yield the right-of- way on his road.

Percy decided to take a step forward. The moose did not seem pugnacious. It would probably spook and head for the trees. He moved toward the moose, looking point-blank at the animal's flaccid nose which overhung its mouth.

The moose moved, but not toward the trees. Head down, ears pinned back, with the fur on its back standing, the moose charged.

The cow covered the distance between them so quickly Liebowitz had no time to react. He crumpled like a baby carriage hit by a speeding bus.

The ungulate began stomping, rearing up both front hooves and coming down, narrowly missing Percy's head, striking quick, painful blows to Percy's neck and shoulders. Like a salmon under the claw of a grizzly bear, Percy could only gasp mutely.

The old man just managed to bring his arms up in a weak attempt to protect his head. Having gotten himself into this mess, he was too embarrassed to scream. He was just hoping the moose would stop before someone happened by to see him this way, so defeated, so, undignified. When the beast came down simultaneously with both front hooves on the old man's temple, his cranium burst and Percy Liebowitz's brain activity ceased. His body would not be found for several hours.

CHAPTER TWENTY-THREE

When Jim arrived at Moss's, Jess Jester was there ahead of him, talking to Sam in front of the log cabin. Bruno parked, killed the tool truck's engine and gathered up his gloves, Thermos and lunch. Then he opened the truck door and headed over to where the two stood.

"Howdy, Jimbo. What's Ed's status?" Jess asked him.

Jim winced. "Not good. They had to amputate his foot last night. They're not sure, but they think maybe his insides aren't burned too bad. I'll know more when I go in after drilling today."

Annie came out to the porch while Jim was talking. She was in her robe and had her arms wrapped around herself.

Jim looked at her. "Annie, I want to thank you. Doc White told me you saved Ed's life. To repay you, I'm going to stick this out and get you some water, no matter what."

"I appreciate that Jim. But Sam and I talked about this last night and we decided we don't want anyone else getting hurt over this, even if it means not having water." She was fighting tears. "If it's not safe, we want you to stop."

God, she is tough, Jim thought.

"It's okay. I'll get it."

He and Jess looked at each other then started toward the drill rig. Sam and Annie chose to stay behind. Halfway there, Jester, true to his name, tried to lighten things up.

"Things been going just smooth as lightning for you here lately, huh Jimmy?"

"Yep," Jim answered quickly, trying not to sound sorry for himself. As Jess and he got closer to the rig, Jim recognized a feeling he did not normally associate with work: apprehension. He felt fear. For the first time ever, James R. Bruno was afraid to go to work.

They timidly approached the spot where Ed had been hurt yesterday. In the shadow of the rig, Jester's thin face appeared drawn and taut. Jim was not at all his usual straight-postured, chest-out, confident self. Both men looked down at the small patch of scorched earth, flesh and blood on the ash-laden moss.

Jim went for a shovel. He did not want to look at that all day. Jester gave the welder a tentative once over, then throwing caution aside, pulled out a crescent wrench and unbolted the cover. Jim watched over his shoulder. The big driller glanced up to the house for signs of movement. It was doubtful coffee and muffins would be forthcoming today. The customers usually became increasingly scarce the deeper the well went.

Since arriving for work, Jim Bruno crossed over the line that separated fortitude from fear. Jim began forcing himself to visualize Ed in his hospital bed. The perspective put him in an entirely different emotional playing field. Better to be mad than afraid, in a game like this.

"Holy Shit, Batman!" Jess yelped.

Jim moved in closer and saw the melted insulation that once covered the main power feed from the generator side of the unit.

"It wasn't the volts that got him, it was the amps and all this wet ground around here. He got all 200 amps." Jess backed up his statement by pointing out the dead short hot lead wire that was touching the welding machine's frame. It had nearly a foot of insulation melted away, exposing a braided copper-wire killer.

"What caused that, Jess?" Jim asked the handyman.

"No idea. You guys haven't done any pipe thawing lately?"

Jim shook his head, no.

"I don't know what else could cause enough resistance to create that kinda heat." Jester was perplexed.

"Can you get it going for me, Jess?"

"1 can requisition some new wire and replace the culprit, but if the winding is fried, you kin forget it."

"I'm just going to drill open hole without casing it today, so I won't need the welder unless something breaks. I'll be shutting down early today. It'd be easier for you to work on it then, without the rig shaking and pounding."

"Roger that, Jimbo! I'll be back here at sixteen hundred hours. You want me to remain on standby for awhile?"

"Naw, take off. I'll be all right," Jim said, hoping he was right. "Jess, leave the old wire here in case OHSA wants to look at it."

"Ten-four." Jester's eyes wrinkled at the corners in concern. He patted his big friend on the upper arm and left.

Jim walked with gingerly trepidation around the rig looking for... what? He didn't know. Booby traps maybe. He climbed the derrick, checked all the cable, pins and pulleys. He half expected something to reach out and grab him when he hit the start button on the engine, but nothing did. The motor revolved twice and brought the rig to life with a small smoke signal of silver-black exhaust. He let out a breath of relief. Okay so far. Jim went to the rear controls at the back of the drill rig and throttled it down. Standing there alone, Jim wished he'd gotten the opportunity to speak with professor Alton before drilling today.

He walked to the truck cab where the ear muffs, hard hats and various hand tools were kept. The clipboard with the well log attached to it was also there. Why had Ed started the welder anyway? They'd agreed not to run anymore casing until they hit some water. Maybe the log would explain.

He reached for the clipboard then looked to the house. No Sam yet. Turning his attention to the log he scanned it until his gaze froze halfway down.

WELL CONSTRUCTION LOG

Driller JB/TYSON ___ Type of rig 22-W ___ Date well completed ___

Well Owner MOSS ___ Nearest community ANCHOR POINT

Well location: (address & legal description) END OF PEGGY STREET / LOT 1 BLK 8 THOMPSON SUB.

Depth of well ___ ft. Casing: length 85' 6 ft. diam. 6 in.

Static water level ___ ft. (above below) land surface. Date: ___

Finish of well: (open-end, screen, perforated, open-hole, other) ___

Describe intervals and size: GRAVEL / SAND / CLAY

Well yield tested by (pumping, bailing, air) at ___ gal/min.

for ___ hours with ___ ft. of drawdown from static level.

DRILLER'S MATERIAL LOG

Depth below land surface in feet	Give description of strata penetrated (size of material, color, hardness of drilling, and water content)
0 to 8	TOPSOIL
8 to 25	SAND + GRAVEL
25 to 28	GRAVEL W/WHITE PUMICE STONE
28 to 35	BROWN SANDY CLAY
35 to 52	GRAY CLAY W/ROCKS
52 to 85	GRAY CLAY & SAND
85 to	SOFT BROWN SANDSTONE
to	
to	
to	
to	
to	
to	
to	

"White pumice stone? What the hell was that?" Jim all but said aloud. Ed hadn't mentioned anything about it. But that was not unusual for Ed, the silent one. Jim recalled he was in Ninilchik for that portion of that first day of drilling.

Setting the clipboard back on the seat of the truck, Jim returned to the well. He began cautiously skirting the edges of the bailed slurry trail, moving along head down, looking for this "white pumice." There it was. Like driftwood along a riverbank were the white fragments Ed described in the log. Picking one up gave Jim a chill. Scrutinizing the chips, it only took Jim a second to realize this was not pumice stone. He didn't want to deliberate much more about what this stuff actually was.

He picked up a Pepsi can from the trash pile and tore it in half and threw one half back, keeping the other half. He picked up a few more pieces of the white chips, placing them in the half-Pepsi can for the trip to town later.

Inside the house, Sam winced hearing the sound of the drilling rig being engaged. Even though he knew Jim was out there, for some reason he hadn't anticipated the change in sound. From an idling engine to the spinning metal whine of the big reel rapidly lowering the drill stem. He knew from the events of the past week, very soon now the pound-growl would begin.

Once upon a time the big yellow machine was a welcome sight, after hauling all those damn five-gallon buckets and making all those trips to the outhouse. All those years.

Now, however, the shaking noisy, snapping, rattling, pounding, growling rig was annoying, overbearing and obtrusive. The more it pounded and growled, the more of a drain it continued to be. The further in debt they went, the more despondent they became. The greater chances were that they would have to sell the place they had worked so hard to keep. In the beginning of this project Sam would have scoffed at any of these possibilities.

"You were kinda rough last night, what gives?" Annie asked him, although she already knew the answer.

Sam didn't say anything.

"Aren't you going to talk to him?" They were finishing breakfast. The question was actually a strong suggestion.

Annie was right, he knew. He could argue and lose or just do the right thing, hard as it was.

"Yeah. I'll be back in a minute."

She laid an arm along the top of his back, kissed him lightly on the cheek and headed for the sink with a handful of dishes.

Sam reluctantly put his hand on the peg that protruded through the bear-proof door. The block slid with a clank, freeing the door to open.

Plodding down to the rig like a horse going downhill, Sam broke into the clamorous perimeter of tension around the operation. To his dismay, he suddenly realized he hadn't brought Jim any coffee.

Jim backed away from the rig noise so they wouldn't have to shout. The rig kept pounding, seemingly on auto drill.

"Would you like some coffee?" Sam asked, embarrassed

"No thanks, I brought a Thermos today. Maybe I should offer you some?" Jim tried to sound more cheerful than he felt.

Sam simply raised a hand, shook his head, no.

"You know, a lotta folks around town are hoping for us to give up out here." Jim said to Sam as though they were in collusion.

He definitely had Sam's attention. "What do you think, Jim?"

"I think it would have been better to be born rich instead of good-looking," Jim answered in a feeble attempt to lift Sam's spirits. Failing miserably, he continued, seriously now. "I'll be down past 200 feet today. From that point on there is no charge for the drilling if we don't hit anything."

For the first time Jim was acknowledging out loud the possibility this well could end up dry.

"Thanks, Jim. We appreciate that." Sam was so solemn. "Anything seep in overnight?"

Jim moved his head side to side in an almost imperceptible no.

"Oh well." Now Sam was grinning, trying to keep a sense of humor with the obvious pun. "We'll both be here all day if you need anything."

"Okay. Thanks. I'll be leaving early today. I have to be in Homer by four." If something doesn't wipe me out before then, Jim thought to himself.

Sam simply lifted a hand in combination of affirmation and "see you later." He went back up to the cabin to tell Annie the semi-good news that the most they would pay for a dry hole was the first 200 feet.

Jim was down to 210 feet by lunch time, still in the sandstone. He ate his sandwich then got out the grapefruit. He didn't really like them but his mother back in Boston used to always try to get him to eat grapefruit. He continued to eat them for her sake to this day. He started peeling earnestly, determined to eat it. The thick skin and fruit inside always suggested to him pulling back a scalp to expose a brain. They didn't even taste very good. Preoccupied, without conscious effort, he ate the whole thing, surprising himself.

At three o'clock Jim was still alive. Everything had gone smoothly enough, although a couple of times during the day Jim felt like there was someone or something with him. Twice he had stepped back from the rig, pulled out his ear plugs and looked around. But he only saw a large raven, floating by the top of the hill at eye level, powered by updraft, unmoving except for tail feathers ruddering its flight path.

Big Jim shut the rig down. This was his favorite time of day, not because it was Miller time but because he could finally put his guard down. Or could he? Shit. This job was making him mental. Down 230 feet and nothing, damn!

Driving through Anchor Point, the town looked conspicuously vacant. The one guy in town everyone eventually needs for one of life's most basic essentials, Big Jim Bruno, was in danger of becoming persona non grata in Anchor Point. The town he'd been busting his butt in for the last few years.

Would he be a hero if he got water at Moss's? Arn would still be dead, his body yet to wash ashore somewhere. Ed's prosthetic foot would be a brutal reminder of the well from hell. What about Smokey Joe Widdecomb? After all, he witched it. People usually forgot that, though. Once the witcher left a location, anything that happened after that was the driller's fault.

What about the community water system turning to saltwater? He doubted he was going to be able to fix that. Come to think of it, why hadn't the mayor been all over Jim to work on it? Besides calling and leaving a message on Jim's answering machine saying the service board had approved the work, he had been uncharacteristically quiet about it. Maybe J. T. figured Jim had enough problems and decided to give him a day or so. Not like ol' Bantam to do that, though. Jim made a mental note to check and see if Stinky Pete still had it pumping.

Bruno rounded the corner of the crest of Bay Hill which provided the postcard view of Homer and the Spit below. Some tourists, out of their motor home, posed arm-in-arm at the scenic turnout for a photo. The Spit's east side was lined with the glistening whiteness of waves breaking along the shoreline. Jim would be at the college in less than ten minutes. He looked down at the speedometer to see his speed had slowed to an almost embarrassing rate. He applied pressure to the worn-down pedal, overcoming the subconscious dread he had within him. He did not want to hear the professor say he knew of nothing that would help. Nor was he looking forward to the look of sorrow on the face of Ed's mother at the hospital.

The tool truck rattled to a stop at the front of the converted post office that now housed the South Peninsula Community College. When the new, bigger post office was constructed the college moved in and adapted so nicely there was no hint left that the building had ever been anything but a school. The gray paint was still in good condition. The windows and roof line were trimmed in Congo red and gave the place a museum quality. The high roof was split-level, with skylights between the top of the lower roof and the bottom of the upper roof.

Jim did his customary brush and shake before going inside with the half Pepsi can of "pumice" fragments. Going through the double doors he entered one huge main room with a high ceiling going up to the skylight. The room was half filled with office cubicles. The other portion was taken up with rows of computer terminals. A little voice told Jim to quit procrastinating and sign up for a beginning computer class while he was here.

The phrase "it's all done by computer" always grated on Jim whenever he heard it. There wasn't much use for a computer on a drill rig. What will computer-dependant people do when the power goes out?

There were numbered doors around the perimeter of the big room, apparently leading to classrooms. Standing there looking around the room in dirty work clothes with the ripped half of a Pepsi can in one hand, Jim must have looked very out of place, like a convict at a bar mitzvah. Without waiting for him to come over, the receptionist called loudly to him from across the lobby.

"May I help you, sir?" She calmly demanded an answer.

"I hope so. I'm Jim Bruno. I have an appointment with Professor Alton at four o'clock." Jim looked at the big clock on the wall. He was ten minutes early.

She relaxed her large frame, shifted in her chair and touched her hand to the back of her done-up hair. Smiling now, she pointed. "Room 103. Go right in."

Jim walked in the direction she had indicated. He found the metal door marked "103-Anthropology" and opened it without knocking. Immediately he assumed he'd entered the wrong room. The person sitting behind the desk in no way bore a resemblance to the rich deep voice of authority he had spoken with on the telephone yesterday.

No, this guy looked more like the local version of Danny DeVito.

Nearly everyone in Alaska over the age of twenty-one hails from somewhere else. Then they either become very wealthy or learn to look like a local. Looking local is accomplished by dressing down: putting on breakup boots, a flannel shirt, jeans and a flaky hat, scarf or other one-of-a-kind accessory. Driving a dirty Subaru station wagon with rusted-out fenders also helps.

Alton looked local enough to be a cannery worker. His appearance helped put Jim at ease. He'd been expecting a white-collar stuffed-shirt type.

Jim approached through the obstacle course of haphazardly arranged desks, computers and tables littered with dusty pieces of pottery. Some of the tables had models of old Native villages. Others supported cutaways of caves and dwellings.

The professor rose, extending a hand — a short journey for the squat, compact man.

"You, of course, are Mr. Bruno." Yep, right room.

"Glad to meet you, professor. I sure hope that you might be able to help me." Jim tried to sound as earnest as possible.

"Please sit down." Professor Alton motioned to the chair directly to the right of the desk. Jim felt like he was back in high school. The room smelled of chalk and old dust.

Deeply clearing his throat, the professor asked, "I hope you won't mind if I continue to eat my very belated lunch while we chat?"

"No, go ahead. I'm not hungry," Jim lied politely.

Apparently Professor Alton had the constitution of a grizzly bear. On the desk in front of him was half a Polish dog and a pile of pepperocini stems he was chasing with a Jolt cola. Waiting for the teacher to finish swallowing, Jim took the opportunity to look around the classroom.

Maps picturing Alaska towns and villages as they were long ago, before the arrival of the white man, decorated the upper third of one wall. A current map of the Kenai Peninsula stuck with different colored pins from Ninilchik down hung from another wall, much lower than the other maps. Big Jim hadn't noticed before now how much of the peninsula the Harding Ice Field and its glaciers enveloped. It seemed most of the Kenai mountains were ice-bound. Only the glaciers that came down as rivers of ice to meet Kachemak Bay were visible from Homer, not the ice field itself. A row of windows faced Main Street, dust rising with every passing car. Above the windows, magnificent Eskimo masks were hung, looking down at him indifferently. A larger, more intricate headdress, possibly a chief's, was hung over the door through which he entered.

The archaeologist had so far seemed the pragmatic and articulate type. Normally that would intimidate Jim, but Alton was hardly meticulous with his Polish dog, maintaining his local edge by taking large bites that bulged his cheeks as he chewed. The stocky man's head was large in comparison to his body, but at least his ears didn't stick out to the sides from his nearly hairless scalp. Alton's teeth were stained dark. His intense sapphire-blue eyes detracted from the wrinkles and bags under them. Jim guessed the professor had recently had a fiftieth birthday or was close to it.

The room was quiet. Only muffled car sounds and other city noises could barely be heard though the windows. Professor Alton dabbed at the corners of his mouth with a napkin. "You mentioned certain... peculiarities that have occurred at the site of the Thompson dig. Can you elaborate?"

Jim began his narration with Arn's death the day they started drilling and proceeded to Augustine's eruption and continued sequentially to Ed's accident. Professor Alton listened attentively without interrupting, occasionally running his fingers over his head through his nonexistent hair.

Until now, Alton had successfully ignored the bottom half of the Pepsi can Jim Bruno placed on top of the desk when he first sat down twenty minutes ago. Once Jim finished with Ed's description of the "white pumice" in the well log the professor's eyes went instantly to the beheaded can.

"May I assume that is what we have here?" Alton asked, pointing to the can with all the fingers of his left hand.

"Yes. I was hoping you could analyze them and give me an opinion. I know this sounds crazy, but since this stuff started happening out there everyone in Anchor Point thinks I'm up against some kind of ancient curse or talisman's spell."

Bruno stopped mid-sentence, exasperated. He felt himself crossing the line from credibility to fallacy. The professor put on some bifocals that were hiding amidst his lunch and poured the content of the can into his hand. "Talisman, no. But a shaman, possibly."

Alton surprised Jim by playing along with this improbable theory. When Jim arrived he hadn't been sure if Professor Alton would lend it any credibility.

"These are bone fragments," Alton said convincingly. Using a courtroom tone, he asked Jim, "At what depth did the log indicate these were encountered?"

"Somewhere between twenty-five and thirty-eight feet."

"If I recall correctly, the bluff out there is about thirty to forty feet in height, isn't it?"

"Pretty close to that, yes."

Excitedly, the undersized professor got up, fragments in hand, forcing his chair backward with the insides of his knees. His stubby legs ambled over to a microscope under one of the windows. He picked one of the larger pieces out of his hand and put the rest into a petri dish. Installing the fragment under the lens of the microscope, Alton lifted his glasses up to rest on his forehead. He squinted his left eye closed and peered down into the scope with his right. A phone was ringing outside the classroom door, unanswered.

"Yes. Definitely human. Possibly even a portion of lower vertebrae."

"Can you tell how old it is?" Jim asked hopefully.

"Not without carbon dating." Alton brought his head up from the scope. "Mr. Bruno, I have something to tell you. Come." He beckoned the immense well driller back to the chair by the desk, returning to his spot behind what was left of his lunch. He scooped up everything with a loud crumpling of paper, cardboard and aluminum, swung his arms out as though they were a boom on a crane then let go with both hands over the trash can.

Both men were seated now, educator/scientist and contractor/prospector. Professor Alton pulled a thick manila file from his desk drawer and placed it on his desk where lunch had just been. He laid his glasses down slowly. After pinching the bridge of his nose he began speaking, almost lecturing.

"There exists a legend, three hundred years old, about a vicious shaman who lived originally in Point Hope on the Arctic Coast. I have been researching his life for years in hopes of publishing my findings. After coming up against dead ends on what happened to him after he was banished from Point Hope, I've basically given up."

"Who was this shaman?" Jim asked perplexedly.

"His name was Yaku."

For some reason the name Yaku made Jim as cool as if a window had been opened in January. The bone in his back frosted, his shoulders rocked involuntarily.

The concise professor opened the manila folder. "This is going to sound outrageous, so please remember, you came to me."

Jim nodded, thinking, "Oh, brother."

"What I have discovered through research, interviews conducted in the bush and findings in the Native Archives section of the Museum of Natural History in Fairbanks indicates..." Alton paused, his stubby fingers shifting through the stack of papers, "When a shaman served his community he could gain real authority and supernatural powers in the process. He was one of the few other than the village elders or the chief that was allowed more than one wife. He was capable of directing his power to cure the sick, assist whaling efforts, influence weather, predict the future, and settle disputes between villages. A shaman practicing the dark powers could give others illnesses, bad fortune, even death. Witchcraft, however, was not a constant threat in the daily lives of ordinary villagers.

"One of the most powerful tools used by the shaman was a 'kikituk.' This powerful killer of men is represented here." The professor pushed a photo across to Jim. "This is a wood carving of the supernatural monstrosity. As you see, it had four short legs and an overabundance of extremely sharp teeth. The power of a kikituk was likened to a short-range shotgun blast by the first whites to ever reach the north slope villages in the mid-1800s.

Jim was staring at the photograph, temporarily mesmerized. He knew it was wood, but he couldn't shake the feeling of evil looking at him from those dark eyes. "This is creepy, professor," he said.

Alton continued, determined to give Jim the entire history. "It gets worse... A shaman who possessed such a spirit kept it dormant within his body. When the kikituk was needed the shaman grew 'pregnant,' gestating as a woman does only much faster, usually a matter of days, then gave birth to his horrid offspring. In one recorded instance, a shaman sent one such kikituk to kill another rival shaman in the same village. After the victim's murder the successful shaman coaxed the kikituk back from the dead man's tent and eventually ate and swallowed it, keeping it idle until its services were needed again."

"Was this shaman... Yaku?" Jim had to ask. "Were you looking for him at the Thompson dig?"

"Yes," the professor again ran his hand over his bald head. "He was cast out of the village by the elders for the killing, even though it left them without a medicine man. According to the archives, Yaku left with one wife and his two children. They went due south; the last sighting of them was in the Yukon River area of the interior. I have been digging all over Alaska for his final destination. He is the main subject of my dissertation, 'Primordial Medicine Men of the Upper Northern Hemisphere.' Searching, that is, until now."

"You're not suggesting we drilled into Yaku's stomach and when we weren't looking this little kikituk bastard crawled up the casing or hitched a ride on the bit and is out running around loose raising hell at my customers' place, are you?" This was too much.

The professor brought his left hand up under his sizable chin, resting his head on his thumb and forefinger looking thoughtful and bemused. "That does seem a bit remote, doesn't it?

"A kikituk wasn't the only means of wreaking havoc and injury available to a shaman. The medicine men and shape changers then and even today use many different spells, curses and help from deities to achieve whatever outcome they desire to solicit."

Both men sat staring at the photo, silent as shrews beneath a passing owl.

Jim chose his words carefully. "Professor, don't get me wrong. I am very grateful for all this information. Can you tell me what I can do to stop this curse? I'm going back out there tomorrow to, hopefully, get those folks some water. But I won't be able to keep my mind on the job at hand if I'm worried about some witch doctor or some little shit with sharp teeth popping out from under the rig and biting me in the ass."

"Hmmm.... Yes, I see your dilemma. However, I do think you have stumbled onto Yaku or a curse of his, an old one, and should avoid returning to the site and evacuate your customers. Barring that, I'm afraid I am not certain what countermeasures are available to us. You see, after all this time, I never really expected to find Yaku's burial site alive with curses.

Great. "Well, besides getting water out there, I've got a score to settle," Jim said brazenly, much more so than he actually felt.

"I do know that shamans would give potential victims of other shamans amulets to wear for protection if they suspected an attack or curse was about to be launched in their direction. But that would only help protect you, not destroy the curse."

"Do you have any of those... amulets?"

"No. They were specifically designed for the individual about to be tormented."

Wonderful. This just gets better all the time, Jim lamented to himself.

Alton held up both hands, fingers extended. "Say. I've got a great idea." Reaching for the phone, he punched a series of numbers and waited.

"Extension 217 please."

Evidently no one was there. He hurriedly hung up and dialed again. This time he perked up.

"Millie? Hello? It's Dan." He paused. "Fine? And you?... That's good. Say, is Ben at home?... Millie, it's urgent he call me as soon as he gets in. I'll be in my classroom for another hour, then home... Yes. Very well... You too, Millie, and thank you." He hung up.

"Ben Jamison is an associate of mine that teaches at the University of Alaska, Fairbanks. He has been overseer on several substantial digs above the arctic circle. I participated in two of them. That was when I first became interested in finding and cataloging Yaku. I think Ben will know just where we could reach a practicing shaman in one of the villages on the north slope of the Brooks Range. In fact, possibly more than one, and which one would be best suited to help us."

That was the second time he used the word "us" that Jim noticed. "You mean one of these shamans would come down here?" Jim felt a glimmer of hope.

"Yes. It is my understanding that, want to or not, they would be duty-bound to do so." He paused to bite on the tail of his glasses. "I'll tell you what. I'll explain the situation to Ben tonight and call you with whatever he suggests we do. I wouldn't be surprised to see Ben Jamison himself come down."

Jim gave the professor a business card. After the professor glanced at it, Bruno got up extending a hand. "Thanks for everything, Professor Alton. I'll be home awaiting your call after a stop at the hospital."

Looking up at the towering driller across the desk the professor simply offered, "Call me Dan."

The tone implied a confidence between them, an alliance. Two unlikely partners combined out of necessity, driven by two completely differing personal agendas.

Jim bumped into Dr. Dan at the nurses' station on his way to Ed's room. Number 230.

Figures.

The doctor explained that Ed had been awake only briefly, but he responded well to a check of his nerves and reflexes. Yes, he was aware of the loss of the foot and seemed to take it fairly well, considering he was lucky to be alive. Ed asked about Jim and Dr. Dan told him Jim had been in to see him. He complained of the pain and was given something that would probably keep him out until late tonight or early tomorrow. The surgeon from Anchorage left to go back home. Ed's mother was fogged in at Sea-Tac. Yes, he would tell Ed that Jim had been here again.

Leaving the hospital, Jim knew it was reproachable to be relieved at getting off the hook, not having to deal with Ed, his mom, and their loss. This would give him another full day to come up with something at Moss's. God, he couldn't remember ever wanting to hit water so badly! It would help to bring good news back with him when he came to see Ed. Or would Ed even care?

CHAPTER TWENTY-FOUR

Yaku was being consumed by his fierce, vehement need for retaliation. The cavern lining, shrouded behind thick darkness, absorbed his screams of rage unsympathetically.

"You bastards! I curse you! Do you hear me? I curse you for all of eternity!" He listened for a reply; there was none. For the first time since his parents died, Yaku was losing control. He wanted to see again. The blood covering him began to dry and cake, stretching the skin on his cheeks, forehead and arms. Touching the cave floor around him until finding the body of his wife, Yaku moved his hands gradually up the motionless torso to the battered skull. The shaman's hands slowly traveled from her wounds to his face and back again, dabbing tepid blood on himself. The smell and coppery taste soothed him. His skin relaxed as it was remoisturized.

The cavern was unearthly quiet. The only sound was Yaku's accelerated breathing, air pumping loudly from lungs through nostrils. Yaku held his breath and began to concentrate. His mind must be totally, completely focused. Chanting now in a great exhale, Yaku worked; only his deity could provide him a link to the Evil One, Shurok.

Under normal circumstances Yaku would never have petitioned Shurok. He had been warned by Anuk, "The Great and Wise One," of the price a shaman pays for doing so. He had been taught by the wise Anuk how to *avoid* contacting Shurok. But now, with his death moments away, he would summon his deity and risk requesting an audience with Shurok. The evil one could simply kill him just for asking if the request were deemed unworthy.

Yaku had nothing to lose, magnificent vengeance to gain. The shaman was confident his deity would grant his wish to meld with his kikituk. Yes, his deity will unite them as one. It would be the only way to survive the disrespect the thralls had shown by burying Yaku alive.

To curse the thrall land, sea, and all animals as no Shaman had ever dared ask, "The Evil One" would surely demand his soul, his very essence. Yaku would give it gladly, without hesitation for the chance to bring ruin to the weak and their land. They will pay. They will beg for mercy. He could imagine their cries. Feeble thralls! They will grieve this day, denying his chance to conquer and rule as master over all.

Total concentration. His petition must be precise. Chanting louder, rocking in rhythm with his singing, Yaku clenched his amulet tightly in both hands. The cave became cool and he was unable to sweat. But he could do it. He will give his life, his existence. He and the kikituk will be one. Then together they will wait, dormant, in hibernation at less than basal metabolism to be freed from this tomb. Yes, they will wait.

CHAPTER TWENTY-FIVE

Jim arrived home with a six-pack and a bag of jerky. Barn was there to greet him, watching over the driveway. Once on the front porch, he didn't go inside. Jim set the beer down next to one of the canvas deck chairs, left his coat on and sat down, despite the cold. He fished out a piece of beef jerky for himself and one for the grateful companion that lay beside him.

The sea, tumescent, looked dark and restless, churned in irritation, as if wanting to get at him. The volcano St. Augustine was completely obscured by massive black-bottomed clouds. Jim leaned over the side of the chair, pulled a beer up by its neck and twisted off the cap. Tipping the bottle bottom up he swallowed half the contents. Nothing to do now but gnaw on jerky with ol' Barn dog until the professor called. He decided against checking the answering machine. It was doubtful anything would be on it. Anyone needing a service call probably called one of his competitors. With all that happened, Jim didn't blame them for being frightened.

Finishing the beer, he returned the bottle to the empty square but did not open another. It just didn't taste as good as it usually did after a day's work. He got up to go inside, opened the front door and with one hand on the knob looked down at Barn. The dog, sensing Jim's low spirits, opted to head home.

"That's probably a good move, Barn. See ya later," Jim said to the dog's tail which was swaying away from him.

Jim freed his feet from their steel-toed enclosures one at a time by placing the toe of one foot on the heel of the other while balancing jerky, six-pack and himself against the doorjamb. He furnished the refrigerator's interior with the beer then began uprooting three pork chops from their nearly permanent residence in the meat drawer, along with a couple of roommates, red potatoes. The phone rang its bell. Before answering, Jim tilted his head toward the clock on the wall.

Six thirty. Man, that professor doesn't lollygag much, does he? Jim mused.

"Anchor Point Drilling," he announced into the mouthpiece. Jim would say that in place of "Hello" during business hours or if he suspected an incoming work-related call. This time he was doing it to impress the professor.

Bruno's ear anticipated Alton's deep baritone. His mind formed a picture of the man's big head and thick black beard.

But instead of the rich voice of confident authority Jim expected, an unconvincing scratchy drawl said, "Jimbo? It's Smokey Joe. How are ya?"

"Fine, Joe, what's up?" This was a surprise.

"How ya doin' out t' tdat well north a town?"

Hesitant concern enveloped Smokey Joe's words, sounding more deliberate and uncomfortable than he normally did. Jim now regretted the ambivalence he'd been feeling toward Joe since Ed had been hurt.

"Nothing yet, Joe."

"Are ya goin' t' be out deya tamorrah?"

"Yeah, I'll be there first thing." Jim wanted to say, "Why do you ask?" but decided to wait him out.

"Jim ah'd like t' come out 'n' witch that again, no charge."

"How come, Joe?" he asked, noticing now how warm he was. Jim wiggled his clay-stained work jacket coat from his shoulders.

"Sumpin' weren't right dere."

That's a no-shitter, thought Jim.

"Okay, Joe, what time?"

"Be deya 'round eleven ifn dat's all right whit you."

"That's fine, Joe. See you then." The two men hung up.

That was interesting. Joe Widdecomb never made it out before noon. Either Joe's conscience finally got to him or maybe ol' Smokey Joe somehow knew what was cooking between Jim and Professor Alton. If Alton's friend can scrounge up a voodoo chief and Joe comes out tomorrow, we might actually figure out what the hell is going on.

Thinking some sort of definite conclusion was near got Big Jim excited enough to open another Michelob. He economized his pacing movements by turning on his ugly clock radio. He needed to know what the weather would be doing tomorrow. After a few minutes of news the announcer on KBBI began telling his listeners about an Anchor Point man who suffered a serious electric shock while drilling a water well for a local contractor at a site just north of Anchor Point, at mile 157. He went on the say that Ed Tyson, age 26, was in serious but stable condition at South Peninsula Hospital.

Hearing the news story like that in black and white made Ed's loss even more real. It validated that it really happened. God. This would be on the Kenai stations and in the Anchorage Daily News. Not the kind of advertising a guy hopes for.

After the sports and marine weather, the Kenai Peninsula forecast was updated. A monotone weatherman informed him, "Seas to twelve feet. Small-craft advisory issued from Gore Point to Castle Cape. Northeast winds to twenty knots. Continued clouds, rain becoming showers. Tomorrow, gale warnings! Seas eighteen to twenty-two feet, winds to thirty knots."

Continued crappy becoming really shitty. Great. Jim shut it off. He didn't need to hear the rest. The weather inland would be better, but not enough to matter.

Master chef Bruno quartered the potatoes into a cast iron skillet with the chops. Covered by a deluge of mushroom soup, the mixture was soon bubbling away slowly, lava-like, but failing miserably to become savory in appearance. Julia Child would not have been impressed.

After a third beer, Jim ate his own cooking. He left the mess, put on his sweats, and played a Sanborn tape. He leaned back at the table, thinking, and wondering about tomorrow. The bachelor looked out at the darkness he knew to be the ocean. With the dark cloud cover and no moon in the sky, the sea was intangible. His thoughts were drifting like currents when the tide turns; churning one direction, then turning and swirling in another.

The flow of the current gravitated him to Tripoli. His mind pictured the two of them alone, somewhere remote. She, looking up at him, sleepy-eyed and adoring...

The phone brought him back from la-la-land. Gotta be Alton this time!

"Hello." It would be silly to say "Anchor Point Drilling" this late at night.

"Jim Bruno, please." It was Dan Alton all right. The penetrating intensity of his voice was immediately recognizable. Jim felt somewhat slighted that the professor didn't acknowledge his voice as well.

"This is Jim, professor, go ahead."

"Jim, I just this moment got off the phone with Ben Jamison in Fairbanks. We had a most interesting and productive discussion. "

"Does he know of anyone who can help?" Let's cut to the chase, Jim thought impatiently.

"Yes! He personally knows two shape-changers practicing in Kaktovik, and he has a close friend in Nuiqsut who is a medicine man who utilizes the old ways. All three are qualified to help us. He is trying to reach them as we speak. Failing that, he will keep trying tomorrow. However, even if he does contact them tonight, the earliest we can expect to see them arriving here would be late tomorrow night."

The professor's use of "us" and "we" did not go unnoticed by the driller and he appreciated Alton's commitment. But tomorrow night might not be soon enough.

"Dan, I've still got to go out there tomorrow to drill, and the fellow who witched the well is coming out. Did your associate suggest anything we could maybe do before they get here?" Jim almost crossed his fingers.

"Of course, I explained the situation at length to Dr. Jamison and he concurs with my conclusion that you have managed to stumble onto Yaku."

Jim was hit by a wave of dread. He felt like a patient at the doctor's office for another opinion hearing, "Yes, it is malignant," for the second time.

Alton continued, "He has a theory. Jim, I must tell you I have the utmost respect for his opinion. Ben Jamison is the leading authority on Alaska Native history for the time period in which Yaku and his contemporaries lived. His knowledge of shamanism past and present is unequaled."

Jim Bruno managed half a smile. Why are these magna-cum-laude types always so long-winded? Jim also wondered what Alton had eaten for dinner. How could a man so obviously refined and articulate as the professor eat something as undistinguished and chaotic as that lunch Jim had witnessed?

"What did he say?"

"He maintains that Yaku has the entire measure of land under his control by means of a powerful land curse, a never-before-used curse involving the immediate land in your area, the seascape, the animals — even the plant life.

"Whoa, is this guy in touch with reality?" Jim wanted to ask, but didn't.

The professor continued, "In essence, Yaku has instilled a type of malicious tumor on nature in your particular part of the country. This indicates Yaku had been a much more powerful shaman than is widely believed. The recovered historical evidence chronicled in the Native archives must be incorrect." He paused. "The strange thing about this is, if Yaku had been that omnipotent, a handful of villagers could not have exiled him."

Great, super shaman. "Professor, I think you have probably anticipated my next question. How do we break this... nature curse?"

"Destroy Yaku." Alton said flatly.

"You mean, dig him up?" Jim envisioned his persona a la Indiana Jones at the cave's entrance, down at the bottom of the bluff, lit wooden torch in hand, preparing to enter the shaft leading to the evil Yaku.

"Jim, you already have."

CHAPTER TWENTY-SIX

*J*im was standing at the rear of the drill rig, certain water would be forthcoming any minute. Little, if any, doubt remained. He lowered the drill string down the well. Engaging the clutch into drilling mode, he stood motionless, the cable sliding through his hand with each stroke. The big driller felt the action of the bit pounding and the reaction of the formation. Somehow he knew the precise moment he would strike water. The I-beam bumper right below the controls had a bumper sticker he'd never seen before. It read: "WELL DRILLING IS THE ONLY JOB YOU START AT THE TOP!" Did Ed put that there? Where is he? He's going to miss it; I'm about to hit the big water. I know because I am a wise old driller like Fido Tasker. Still no Ed. Alone. Oh, well, here goes.

At the precise stroke which Jim knew would yield water, the sound of rapidly depressurizing gas could be heard at a distance. It was coming from the bottom of the well and was gradually becoming louder. The drill line went slack.

Holy shit!

Disengaging the drilling clutch, Jim quickly switched over to pull the bit and the rest of the tool string out of the hole. He could not catch up! He gave the engine more throttle but he still could not take up the slack. The string was coming up faster than he could reel it in. The bit was being blown up the hole.

Jim continued pulling on the lever, throttle wide open now, spinning the drilling reel faster than it had ever revolved. Jim watched the reel, watched the cable. It was spooling on the drum unnaturally, folding over itself unevenly due to lack of weight. The cable was forming a bird's nest that would never roll back.

Jim decided that by the time the spool got close to being full, if he hadn't caught up to the tool string he would have to bail out. That or risk being crushed by his own drill stem and bit. What was happening? Why was this happening?

Seconds passed. The cable nearly filled the reel. He latched down the brake out of habit. It wouldn't help. It only prevented the bit from going down, not up. He turned and fled. While *doing so he thought, how far? Do I stop or just keep running? Halfway to the cabin he stopped and turned back for a look.*

Cable was spewing from the well and piling up haphazardly around the back of the rig, like spaghetti. The screaming noise was louder now. Jim's hands went over his ears, trying to block out the venting sound to no avail.

Then it came.

The top of the string and the rope socket cleared the casing followed by the stem and bit. Not even slowing down, the bit was spit up, smashing into the derrick and doing considerable damage before falling away. The 2,000-pound stem came tipping down with a loud slap right where Jim had stood prior to fleeing.

Before the stem became motionless, a pinkish gas became visible as well as deafening. While it was being released to the atmosphere the shrill whistle of depressurization subsided as the gas cloud rose vertically, paralleling the derrick. The fog-mist cloud began bulging at its middle, turning from blush pink to dark ruby and then throbbing to pink again. The pulsating gas cloud was changing itself rapidly. It was no longer opaque, taking substantive form. It sprouted arms, a head, but no legs. It became a giant Eskimo genie taller than the rig with dark glowing eyes that brimmed with hate.

The monster looked down at Jim, knowing all there was to know. The genie put a massive hand around the derrick and squeezed, reducing it to one-eighth of its former size in a loud, unrepairable collapse.

The sound of metal collapsing is what jerked Bruno thankfully awake. That and all the work involved in rebuilding a rig derrick.

Whew! That one got him sweating. He wiped away the hair stuck to his forehead and sat upright. Christ! These professor-witch-doctor experts were making him crazy! Jim thought.

"I just gotta hit water today. I can't do another night of this."

It had to be last evening's phone conversations that produced the dream. Jim was remembering now; Joe was coming out today for a rewitch. Why? It was something Joe just didn't do without first being asked.

Last night, Professor Alton called back a second time, going on to explain some of the possible ways Yaku's curse could have been unleashed.

Alton told Jim that Yaku could have metamorphosed into a type of bacteria. Then, after waiting all the years, attached himself parasitically to Jim's drilling tools and hitched a ride to the surface. Once there the bacteria reproduced and evolved, possible melding with Yaku's kikituk.

Another possibility was that Yaku's essence came up with the bone fragments in the drilling-mud cuttings. Alton's friend in Fairbanks, Ben Jamison, firmly rejected that theory, however.

"It is even possible Yaku had melded with his kikituk and remained suspended as an inert gas or mist," Alton suggested.

"You mean like a genie?" Jim was starting to believe anything now. Maybe he should get Aladdin to help finish drilling this well, he joked to himself.

Alton answered with a slight indignation noticeable in his deep voice. "Well, in a sense, yes. That would be consistent with Ben's research. Yaku could not get out on his own, according to the few known legends that refer to 'the nature curse' and this type of circumstance. Ben assumed Yaku became trapped somehow. In that case he must be let out to begin his carnage. It is doubtful Yaku anticipated this length of time passing before being freed."

That was what the man said all right. Jim and Ed let the genie out of the bottle and, boy, was he pissed! How am I gonna explain to the OSHA investigators that Ed was injured by 300-year-old genie vapor? They're going to lock me up and throw the key down a well, thought Jim bleakly. Doubtful the National Guard would help, either. This is that damn Fido's fault for getting me into this God-damn business, Jim thought, but he didn't mean it.

Jim dressed with the feeling pressing him that his days were numbered. Just as well. After today, his resolve would be as dry as that hole in the ground. Nothing else to do but go out there and get western with the son-of-a-bitch.

CHAPTER TWENTY-SEVEN

As he stepped out his front door, the worsening weather conditions caught Jim's eye before the door closed. The inlet water was still shadowed by clouds that formed a battleship-gray wall obscuring St. Augustine and the Alaska Range. Except for peaking whitecaps, the sea was nearly black. Once the dark-bottomed clouds quit threatening and actually moved inland, things would get nasty.

Jim looked in the toolbox to certify his rain gear was still there. He closed the big utility box door and looked up at the treetops. The spruce timber was bending, capitulating to the increasing wind gusts; an evergreen slow dance.

He drove through a ghost town to the gas station for the usual. Only Wrong Way was there today. It was then that Jim found out about Percy Liebowitz's death. Jim knew the articulate old man and liked him. Wrong Way said Percy's head was crushed. Now, driving to work at Moss's, he felt responsible for Percy's brutal demise on top of everything else.

Arriving at eight, Jim went straight to the front door rather than to the drill rig. After knocking loudly, he realized he did not want to see the depressed look occupying the faces inside. After a few seconds the latch slid toward the hinges loudly.

"Good morning, Jim." Annie smiled weakly. The freckles across the bridge of her nose were more apparent this morning. "Come sit down and have some coffee before you start."

"Thanks," was all he could muster. He was trying to determine how to begin telling his customers what he had planned. Jim slid the latch with a clank after closing the big door behind him. Sam was coming down the stairs pulling on a shirt to cover his very white, hairless chest. Sam didn't have the thin, weak-looking physique normally stereotyped with such red hair and pale complexion. Jim could tell that Sam's strength was the kind that came from hard work, not from a gym or country club.

"Hi, Jim." Sam offered an encouraging expression.

Annie brought them each a cup of steaming coffee. No music came from the stereo's speakers this morning.

Jim whistled backward sucking in half air, half coffee, successfully preventing a burned mouth. He set down the cup and began. "I had some very interesting conversations yesterday, heard some pretty wild stuff."

Jim Bruno's two customers listened attentively, unsurprised.

"I went to visit Joe Widdecomb day before yesterday. I wasn't sure, but I thought he acted a little strange the day he witched your well. I decided to go try and get an explanation and also to see if he would say how much farther he thought we should drill." Jim paused for another sip of coffee. While doing so, he looked over the rim of his cup to try and gauge Sam and his wife's reaction. He wondered if they knew about Percy.

"All he would tell me at first was that he was certain there is water down there and we should keep going. Then in a roundabout way Joe gave me the name of an archaeologist who teaches at the community college. I went down and saw him yesterday after I left here. His name is Dan Alton. He was the one that oversaw the dig here in 1977. He feels that, because of all that has happened, you two are in danger if you stay here until we finish drilling. He thought it would be wise for you folks to find someplace else to stay for just a day or two. In the meantime, he has arranged for some specialists to come down and help us figure out what's goin' on here." Jim hoped he'd been vague enough, but not too vague.

"You mean he thinks we're not safe in our own home?" Annie questioned, clearly unconvinced.

"With everything that has been happening around here and now Liebowitz...."

"Percy? You mean Percy Liebowitz down the creek from us? What happened?" Sam asked the driller.

So they didn't know. Guess it's best to just blurt it out.

"He was stomped to death by a moose. Right on his road. His neighbors found him when they came home last night. Pretty bad, I guess." Hopefully that will be enough to convince them, Jim thought.

"We're not going to get stomped by no moose," Sam declared, glancing in punctuation at the gun cabinet containing the rifles and a twelve gauge.

Jim picked it upon it. "Sam, the kind of stuff that's been going on around here, that shotgun wouldn't have prevented."

Sam considered this. He was torn between wanting to keep Annie safe and staying to fight and protect his home. He was not a coward and it did not feel right to leave Jim Bruno here alone to deal with this for him.

"Jim, why did the archaeologist... What is his name?... Alton? Why did he say we are in danger? And what are the people coming down from Fairbanks going to do? Are they some kind of private investigators?" Annie asked Jim pointedly.

She should be scared, Jim thought. Actually, she probably was, but no one could tell it. Such a strong yet lovely woman. Again she was impressing Jim with her inner strength. It was coming through clearly. Sam was a lucky man to have her on his side.

But, boy, oh boy, Jim had hoped to stay vague and get away with not having to try and explain the "nature curse." Having to describe Yaku to someone else would be admitting he believed it himself. Jim wasn't sure he wanted to admit to that yet. Acknowledging Yaku's existence would be terrifying and would make today's project that much tougher to get through.

What the hell, he did his best. Beginning with the "pumice stone" Ed recorded in the well log, then his meeting with Alton, the subsequent phone calls in which Alton and Jamison set up a shaman, maybe two, to arrive late tonight or early tomorrow from one of the North Slope villages.

Toward the end of this explanation, Big Jim was listening to himself speak and was mindful of how crazy it all sounded. He hoped Sam and Annie wouldn't think he had snapped under the pressure. Considering the past few days' occurrences there weren't really too many other readily available explanations.

Finished now, Jim took an unwanted sip of coffee using his cup as a prop. He waited, almost holding his breath, to find out how the Mosses would react to all this. If they bought into it, then he would buy into it too, even if that meant spending the day looking for little red-eyed monsters with sharp teeth.

"So... You drilled right into this guy Yaku and he's gotten loose and put a 'land curse' on us?" Sam asked, looking at Jim hoping he would say no.

He didn't.

"Not just us. If Yaku caused Augustine's eruption and Arn's death, then the whole peninsula could be affected by it," Jim told him.

"We could go down to the boat, but if this 'curse' covers the entire Kenai Peninsula we wouldn't really be safe there either, would we?" Annie looked to her husband after calmly making the statement.

"I think you'd be much better off. The core of it all is right here. I've got a gut feeling that something is going to break loose today. If I have to, I'm going to work late to force the issue. I'd have less to worry about if you folks were away safe somewhere. Too many people have been hurt already." Jim looked to Sam expectantly.

"Jim, I'd like to get Annie out of here but I'm not going to leave you alone to fight this... this... Yaku for me." Sam was adamant.

"I appreciate it, Sam, but don't worry. I won't be alone much. Smokey Joe is coming out to rewitch and Alton's pals will be showing up today, so I'll be all right." Well, they might be any way.

The three of them sat in contemplative silence, staring into their cups as if reading tea leaves.

Jim was thinking back to the first time he sat on this stool. Things were much different now. You could have touched the anticipation. The optimism had been as palpable then as the dread was now.

Sam's stool let out a long low screech when he slid it back, got up, and went across the living room to the gun cabinet. He put his hand around the wooden handle on the glass door and opened it.

If he's breaking out the firearms then he really believes this shit, Jim thought, watching.

The weapons were well-cared for, immaculate even. The stocks were oiled, the barrels all uniformly blue-black and glossy. Ammo and other accessories were stacked neatly at the butt of their related rifles. Without a word, Sam wrapped his fingers around the stock of the twelve gauge, removed it slowly and picked up a box of shells with his left hand. Sam sat down in one of the living room chairs, opened the box and started loading the shotgun. The sanguine-colored shells slid with a smooth, clean metallic clink, clink, clink. He checked to see the safety was on, then carried the weapon over to the big front door setting it down butt first with the barrel leaned against the doorjamb. Sam then went back and got out a rifle and some more shells.

"All right, I don't like it, but we'll go," Sam said with disgust while loading the rifle. "We'll stay on the boat to-night. Jim, take the scatter gun out to the rig with you. We'll take the 30-30. I'll load the .30-06 and leave it in the cabi-net. The house will be open. We'll stop at Roy-Boy's on the way out and ask him to look in on you and lock up after you leave.

"Okay. Thanks, Sam." Jim hadn't considered bringing a firearm to work but it certainly seemed to be a good idea now. The only other times he and Ed carried guns to work were if a brown bear had been harassing the neighborhood, or if it was moose season. And, of course, there was that one memorable job they'd done at Hasty Banana's out the top of the North Fork. Hasty had several large full-grown hogs she let range free on her ten acres. They slept under her cabin, which stood five feet above ground on stilts. The largest of the pigs was a 400-pounder named Ace. Ace was particularly mean and had attacked Hasty only a week prior during feeding time. After Hasty described the attack warning them about Ace, Hasty gave them permission to protect themselves. So every day at Hasty Banana's Ed had a .44 holstered at his side.

Annie poured each man a refill then replaced the dented pot on the top of the wood stove. She headed up the stairs without a word, presumably to carry Out the joyless task of packing an overnight bag.

You'll be able to reach us through the Harbormaster's office. The number is right here." Sam showed Jim the num-ber, one of several written on a thick piece of fish-packing cardboard tacked to the curved log wall. "Call if something comes up."

The two men looked at each other then chuckled morosely.

"We'll be doing odds and ends on the boat all day," Sam told him, although he was forming a different plan for today.

"Sounds good. I'm sure something's gonna give. Be expecting a call." Out of words, Big Jim stood and offered his hand. "Today has got to be it, Sam. I'll get you some water."

Sam just nodded and shook Jim's hand with a firm grip.

God, after all this drama I hope I'm right, Jim thought to himself.

Two minutes later, Jim was walking down to the rig, shotgun in hand like Matt Dillon going down the street for a showdown. He was hoping to remember something he'd forgotten in the pickup but nothing came to mind. Talk is cheap until things actually get hairy. Jim had the urge to fire a round in the rig's direction; a warning shot across the bow, of sorts.

Once at the rig, Jim was reluctant to set the gun down. Yesterday he was afraid. Today he was afraid and downright jumpy. If someone were to pop a paper bag near him right now his heart would probably stop. Jim's nerves were talking.

Slowly, hesitantly, Big Jim leaned the shotgun against a clean spot on a nearby birch tree. He pulled his gloves on and began an inspection of the drill site.

He checked the blocking under the rig jacks, the draw works, cables, engine, the belt drive, and then he climbed the derrick to check all the pulleys and sheaves, braces and pins. All the while looking for that little kikituk bastard with the sharp teeth.

Satisfied, Bruno started the rig engine. It fired; nothing happened. Okay. So far, so good.

Jim walked to the rear of the rig. The drill stem hung just as he'd left it, half in the well, half above ground exposed to prevent anyone from tampering with the well. Lowering the tool string down to the rope socket, Jim examined it for wear or signs of sabotage. There were none. He unlocked the brake and let enough tension off to allow the stem, rope socket and bit to free-fall to the bottom. He watched the cable closely on its way underground for signs of foul play. Fishing for a tool string at the end of 145 feet of open hole could ruin a guy's entire day.

The cable looked to be in good shape. The bit bottomed out right where it should have, according to the last mark

Jim spray-painted on the cable yesterday. Bruno reached down into the bottom of the derrick where the white spray paint was kept. With his other hand he picked up the five-foot stick that was always leaning into the rig's left side. Jim held the stick steady against the cable with the stick's bottom at the top of the last mark, 230 feet. He then sprayed the cable from the top of the stick down about five inches. Once this mark was drilled down to ground level, the well would be 235 feet deep.

Man! *235 feet!* This is getting way deep. That thought lingered, adding another layer of stress to Bruno's already burdened psyche like another inch of snow on a ridge. About to avalanche, he could stand the weight for now, but any loud noises or sudden movements could bring him down.

Bruno heaved back on the lever that engaged the drill-gear clutch.

Pound-Growl... Pound-Growl... Pound-Growl...

He was drilling again. He poured in two five-gallon buckets of water he likely wouldn't see again.

Over the expanse of muskeg and creek bottom that began below Jim at the old caves a flock of geese was forming up for the trip south. They were circling around like biplanes in a World War I dogfight, the elder geese honking and quacking loudly, urging this year's newcomers into line. Jim watched them with some amusement with one hand on the cable feeling the drilling action of the bit over 200 feet below.

After a short time, the geese arranged themselves into a crude form resembling an uneven V. Jim knew that long before they arrived at their final destination the V, out of necessity, would be of perfect proportions. Jim wondered if they'd be as relieved to get there as he would to be to finally hit some water. Did they dread a forthcoming trip or look forward to it? Were they leaving today for the obvious reason or did they know something?

A horn's toot snapped him out of it. He turned his head quickly right, eyes sighting in on the driveway. Sam and Annie were leaving in their pickup. Sam's arm was out the window waving good-bye. Annie was seated next to Sam, the .30-30 clearly visible, set in the gun rack at the back window. Annie's list remained behind on her counter, forgotten.

Jim wasn't the only one watching them leave.

Seeing his customers go without bringing the now traditional coffee down reminded him he'd forgotten his Thermos today. The wind wasn't too bad when he first arrived, but it was picking up now. A wide scattering of raindrops were putting in an appearance. Coffee would have helped fend off the cold. How could he have forgotten it?

In forty minutes Jim had the 235 feet mark two feet below ground level. Time to clean out the hole. Jim let the machine drill without him while he did a little walk around looking for...? What? "Am I paranoid or what?" he asked the drill rig. He had a feeling of being watched, something not quite right. After looking all around, Big Jim pressed his lips together tightly and shook his head. Nobody here but us chickens!

He returned his left hand to the control and kicked the machine out of drill, timing it to disengage on the down stroke. Jim throttled up and pulled hard on the lever controlling the main line, bright blue eyes intently scrutinizing the cable for any sign of moisture on the way up. Soon the top of the drill string broke the surface. Dry. Bummer. Then the bottom of the string cleared the casing. Jim released the main line control lever and simultaneously applied downward pressure on the brake, leaving the twenty-foot-long drill stem hanging.

The mud-sand was up on the bit slightly higher than usual. It seemed a little darker in color than it had been yesterday too.

Jim reached out a gloved hand and pushed the stem an arm's length away and eased up on the brake just enough to gradually set it down. The big driller then locked the brake down hard so the drill stem stood, its rope socket on top pointing to the derrick's crown. It would stand that way without leaning into the rig, as long as the brake held.

The well had Jim's full attention now. A good color change would be welcome indeed. It could mean he was getting close. Unfortunately, it also could be that the formation they'd been drilling in was changing, but staying dry.

Jim lifted the bailer lever, picked up the tool, centered it over the well and sent it down. Free-falling with a metal "sickling" sound, it was allowed to descend much faster than the stem, being a fraction of the stem in weight. If it got hung up or stuck on something it wasn't nearly as tough to get loose as the 2,000-pound stem.

The number of wraps left on the bailer reel told Jim the tool was close to the bottom. He applied pressure on the control to slow the rate of descent. When it landed it hit with a muffled, less resounding clang than it had last time.

It felt like the bailer traveled through two or three gallons of muck before touching down. Not as empty as usual, but nothing to get excited about either. At least it was two or three gallons more than he'd been getting.

Once the driller had the bailer up to the surface again he emptied the contents into the trough. It was definite. The formation was changing color. Same clay/sandstone mix but darker. It changed its appearance from Swiss to German-chocolate mud.

Ten minutes later he marked 240 feet and was drilling, adding water and hoping this was it.

238 feet, 239 feet, the 240 foot mark was going below ground. It was drilling better now.

Over the sound of the rig noise a different tone entered Jim's ear. A low rumbling hum. Worried, he looked quickly to the engine. Over the years good drillers developed an "ear" for the precise correct sound of their machines and the drilling action they create. Any deviation or new noises would get immediate recognition from a proficient operator.

Jim was about to look at the engine's gauges when movement on the Mosses' driveway caught his eye.

The noise was Smokey Joe's Plymouth. Jim squinted down at his wrist and realized Joe was over an hour early. Very unlike Joe to even be up this early. Hmmm... this should be interesting.

It didn't look like Marie accompanied Joe today, also out of the ordinary. She wouldn't have gotten out of the car anyway. She only did so to have lunch at the lodge, which they did religiously whenever they were out witching wells together.

Jim stayed with the rig, letting it continue to drill. It would take Joe a few minutes to get out of the car, get his rods and make it down to the rig.

Once Joe got close, Jim kicked the rig out of gear and raised the stem up safely into the cased portion of the well before idling the engine down. Then he moved the trough, some pipe and the water buckets so Joe could have access to the well free from tripping hazards.

"G'mornin', Jim," Joe said a little sheepishly. His head nodded down toward his breakup boots. Joe had his faded-blue bib overalls on, a clean T-shirt underneath. The brass rods clutched tightly by his right hand hung alongside his leg.

"Joe." Jim shot Joe an austere look, trying to be mad at the old witcher.

He couldn't. Anyway, it was Ol' Joe who had steered him to Professor Alton; and now Joe was here to help without having been asked.

"Anything?" Joe asked expectantly.

Jim shook his head lightly. "I just got into a color change but it's still dry. I'm getting back what I pour in for the first time. That hasn't happened since we were down ninety feet."

Joe stammered. "Well, Jim... the reason... the reason ah come out here, well, ah felt sumpin' real strange t' other day when we's out here witchin'." Joe looked down again. "Ah was afraid t' say anything'. Figgered you think ah finally lost mah marbles."

"Strange? How, Joe?" Maybe now we'll unravel part of this, Jim thought.

"Lemme try it again, would'cha? Den I'll tell ya what I think it was, 'kay?"

Jim nodded approval. What else could he say?

Joe lifted the brass rods up, took one in each hand and began baby stepping toward the well. Three feet from the well the rods crossed into Joe's chest with a light chink! Joe stopped briefly then covered the rest of the distance to the well.

Jim moved to a better vantage point so he could watch Joe's face. Standing there, rods crossed, Joe appeared quizzical, but not at all halted and locked up like he was the last time he witched this well. Jim didn't say a thing; he just waited patiently.

Smokey Joe pursed his lips and bit on his cheek. Lowering the rods he cautiously treaded across the mud returns head down, continuing until he was six feet past the well. Joe turned, lifted the rods and began witching his way back.

Again, just prior to reaching the well, the rods crossed. Joe backed up, moved two steps aside and repeated the procedure. He seemed to be trying to home in on something. Jim continued to watch his perplexed well witcher. Jim's hunch about what was confusing Joe seemed fairly certain now, and Jim, sorry for Ol' Joe, was about to speak when Joe lowered the rods and looked at the big driller.

"Jim, when I witched dis thing the first time 'round I got a real good pull right away, just like I do now. Dey's a lot 'a water deya all right. But right after dat big pull dey was sumthin' else..." Joe hesitated, searching for words.

"Something else? Like what, Joe?" Jim asked, but he knew like what.

"Something... alive."

"Do you mean something in the water, Joe?"

"No. Sumpin' else. It didn't feel good, Jim. Not a' tall. It felt mean. Real mean. Evil like. It wanted to hurt me. Hurt me real bad. It was evil sumpin' fierce, Jim. I never felt nothin' like it. I didn't say nothin' 'cause I figgered you'd think I was offen my rocker fer sure. You know what people say 'bout witchers being short of a full load anyway, and how their elevators don't go all the way to the top floor." The old man paused, ashamed of himself. "I'm sorry, Jim."

"Joe, don't worry about it. I don't blame you for anything that's happened." He put a hand on Smokey Joe's shoulder for emphasis. "So what do you feel here now?"

"Nothin'. I don't unnerstan' it, Jim. All I'm getting now is the water, just the water. Lots of it, too."

The old witcher couldn't see how what he said affected Big Jim Bruno. The driller's expression didn't change. He'd partly been expecting this. But when Joe had said "nothin," Jim's entire chest twisted like a wet towel being wrung out. Without discussing it face-to-face, Smokey Joe Widdecomb, Dan Alton and Ben Jamison had just concurred.

Yaku was out.

CHAPTER TWENTY-EIGHT

Yaku felt an answer to the summoning chant begin to press into him. The power and presence of his deity were very near. The shaman continued chanting, singing praise. His deity must understand what Yaku wants. The shape-changer's god came to him in a vision, shrouded, cloudy, unclear but there. Yaku was becoming weaker with every breath. Eyes closed, Yaku's mouth moved, speaking not words but thoughts. Sweat crawled down his eyelids now, in spite of the cold.

Yaku continued sending the same two messages over and over to his deity. The first was requesting his deity to help Yaku meld with his kikituk. And the second was to be allowed an audience with Shurok, "The Evil One."

Once Yaku received confirmation his requests had been granted, weak and exhausted, barely able to breathe, he passed out. He had shape-changed twice before; once into a crow, to spy on the nursemaid Kivuk. Another time, the first time he ever attempted to shape-change, he killed "The Great And Wise One," Anuk. He had done so by becoming a venomous insect and biting the old man. It had been painful and passing out was welcome.

Something demanded Yaku awake, but he could only recover to partial consciousness.

Yaku had the sensation he was half-man and half-beast. When Shurok manifested before him in the cave, the pinkish fog-shrouded light hurt him in the place that used to be his eyes. He hadn't expected to ever see again and the shock of this light added to his trepidation of Shurok. Initially only a huge outline with broad shoulders and a massive head were visible, silhouetted in the mist which pulsed now and was turning dark red. A terrifying voice forcefully entered Yaku's mind. The voice did not come through Yaku's ears. He still had ears, though they were much different now. No, the voice was clear, direct, and Yaku heard the deep threatening utterance internally, without mistake.

"For what you desire, you will pay with all."

The message was explicit; its meaning unmistakable. Near death, Yaku did not hesitate. His fear was subsiding and he did not cower. He would give his soul, his essence and whatever else Shurok asked in exchange for revenge. Yes. His answer was yes.

Yaku had few other conscious thoughts after reaching his deadly agreement with Shurok. He realized he was no longer a man. Lying on his side, he knew he did not have two legs but four, even though the red light had all but disappeared. And then he felt a lightness, felt himself animate, floating smoke-like. Soon he would be at a barely basal existence. The thing he had become would not be able to dig itself out. He must be freed, as a bear in hibernation is freed by spring. Was he awake now or asleep but dreaming? He could not tell. What an odd sensation. As Shurok's song of doom faded with the light, the last thing he understood was that he was deep in Shurok's debt.

CHAPTER TWENTY-NINE

Jim thanked his well witcher for coming out, accepting Joe's apology without being too condescending.

After Joe's Plymouth left, the drilling continued to improve. When Big Jim cleaned out the hole at 251 feet, he had nearly a full bailer of slurry. For the first time, when he set the bailer down in the trough to empty its contents, there was enough pressure to splash up onto the back of the rig, catching him from the waist down on his coveralls.

Ugh! That stuff came out cold. He was beginning to get sprinkled from above now too, and the wind was increasing its velocity. The trees could be heard submitting to the wind overhead above the rig noise. Jim was shivering, a slight case of gooseflesh developed on his arms, partly from the cold, partly from nervous excitement.

The second trip down with the bailer yielded very little. The well bore had been cleaned out on the first run. But he got much more back than he put in. Something was going on down there. Yep, something was about to give.

This time Jim only poured in one five-gallon bucket of water instead of the usual two. If he got another full bailer after drilling this time it would mean this thing was actually making some water! Right now he'd even take a gallon a minute.

252 feet, 253 feet, 254 feet. At 255 feet the tool string took off. After three strokes the bit was bouncing without touching bottom. Jim grabbed for the brake and loosened its setting to allow more line out with each stroke. Now with each stroke, the reel was turning three or four inches, screeching loudly.

Jim's heart leaped. Is this it? Under any normal drilling circumstance hitting drilling this good would be cause for celebration. But now, at this depth, with this much of the hole open, prudence was called for.

He only allowed the tool string to fall another two feet before disengaging the drill clutch. Jim was being cautious, but also the suspense was killing him.

Big Jim reeled in the main line again, watching the cable with keen interest for signs of water. Blue eyes darted from the line coming out of the well to the main reel with each blink of eyelids.

With one-hundred feet reeled in, the cable became darker. Jim's eyes narrowed like Spiderman's. He stopped reeling to have a look. He set the brake and ran the back of a gloved hand across the cable. Wet. The cable was wet. A rush of adrenaline flowed through the big man. Either something fell in at 100 feet or there was 157 feet of water in this well right now.

Bruno quickly went back to spooling in the main line. "Be there, please be there," he whispered, pleading to whoever was in control of these things. Who? He thought about it for second. Who was he talking to? Himself? The rig? The god of water? Neptune? Or the person or thing that has or hasn't been watching him all day, or whomever it felt like had been watching him all day?

He continued shivering, waiting for the bit to arrive. The cable was still wet and it even had small rivulets running down the braids.

At last the tool stem cleared the top of the casing. It was shining. Dripping wet and clean! Oh, man! Jim made a fist, pulled it in quickly like a backwards punch and cried, "Yes!" His neck and backbone tingled.

Once the bit was safely out of the way, Jim raised the bailer up enough to clear the casing, held it centered over the hole and let it fly. It pinged and clanged at the usual spots on its way down. At about one-hundred feet it slowed with a soft, hollow deep-sounding spluusshh.

Yes! That sound was sweet to Jim's ears. Two seconds later the bailer had bubbled full and was on its way to the bottom again at top speed. Jim could check the flow rate by bailing off the top but he wanted to verify the bottom-hole integrity to see if any of the hole had been lost when the water came in. If he tagged bottom with slightly more cable out on the bailer than he had last time, the Mosses had a well.

He did. Hallelujah! He was down where he was supposed to be with the bailer. "Yes!" the big driller roared once more, not caring who heard, unable to contain his swelling emotion.

Jim brought the bailer up slowly, emptied it in the trough and splashed beautiful sparkling water all over the place. He wasn't cold anymore. The water was clean, frothing, and no sand, another plus.

Five quick round trips just under the surface of the water's static level at 100 feet didn't budge it. Bailing as fast as he could, Jim was unable to lower it. By the time he got back down each time the water was back at the 100-foot level. That meant it was in excess of twenty-five gallons a minute, five times the needs of a normal household.

"Man, she's coming in like a Big Dog!" Jim was starting to enjoy this talking to himself.

Next would come the best part of his job. Telling the customers and all involved that he and Ed hit the "Big Water of All Time," so big he couldn't measure it, not without getting a large capacity pump because he couldn't bail it fast enough.

Ed's face came to him. He pictured the scene. Ed in his hospital bed, with Jim describing how they had gotten 150 feet of water in the well that you couldn't faze with the bailer, possibly the strongest flow the two of them had ever produced. Ed's loss was a tragedy, but at least now it wasn't for nothing.

Then Jim imagined the relief and elation on the faces of Sam and Annie. They'd hug each other. Jim decided he'd go the harbor first, then to the hospital to see Ed and his mother, whether it was visiting hours or not!

Then to the lodge, to buy a round of drinks for whoever was there, to tell the town of his and Ed's victory and accept the town's congratulations. He might even feel brave enough to maybe ask....

UUGGHH!

Jim heard the inside of his head reverberate. The jarring was instantly accompanied by a strong, forceful pain. Long before the next second passed Jim knew something was terribly wrong. Had part of the derrick fallen on him? Jim was thankfully overtaken by a dark unconsciousness. Thankful because Jim's last thought before his eyes rolled back into his head was recognition that this pain would quickly be getting much worse.

A voice grunted over the downed man.

"All for nothing, Bruno! No one will ever know that you got water here."

CHAPTER THIRTY

Guilt nagged at Sam, pacing him all the way to town. Before reaching the harbor, he made up his mind to go back. Annie concurred.

Once he had Annie settled in safe and sound, he would go back. He would ask the hands working on the long liner *Endeavor* docked in the slip next to theirs to watch over her. The *Endeavor's* skipper and Sam deck-handed together years ago and remained friends. Annie, though quite capable of taking care of herself, would be in very good care. Sam reminded himself to stop for coffee and donuts on the way back.

Pulling the pickup into a rare opening next to the ramp, Sam looked through the windshield to view the harbor that lay before them. As always, Sam's eyes lined up directly to his slip to gaze upon his pride and joy, the *Rainbow*.

Sam's heart was not prepared for what it saw.

The float that held the slip of the *Rainbow* was an arena of commotion. His boat seemed to be the epicenter.

In the middle of it all was Jonesy, the harbormaster. He was gesticulating wildly, throwing an arm one way, then turning and yelling, pointing the other arm in a different direction. A harbor employee in one of the city skiffs was at the stern of the *Rainbow* throwing lines. Two others were carrying some equipment toward the fish hold. Reaching up to receive the equipment out of the hatch were two of the deckhands from the *Endeavor.*

Sam's eyes darted up to the mast. Immediately he knew what the problem was. The *Rainbow* was sinking.

CHAPTER THIRTY-ONE

After muttering to the unconscious driller words obviously unheard, Jake Bantam put the blackjack away with a grin of satisfaction between his fat cheeks. The weapon was a holdover from his days as a bouncer on Anchorage's notorious Fourth Avenue; an invaluable tool in situations where telltale markings were unwanted.

The bald man barked and grunted orders to his swamper without taking his eyes off Jim Bruno. "Take the four-wheeler back to the pickup, then haul ass back here with six bags of the P-mix I brought. I'll take care of him."

With that dispatch, J. T. looked at Darrell Klepesen to ensure that the level of Darrell's understanding was sufficient. Amazingly, it was.

Darrell was just grateful to be leaving. The road time on the four-wheeler to where his boss parked the truck would give him the opportunity to smoke a joint.

Darrell had been hiding just past the clearing where the Mosses' cabin stood, concealed by shadows beneath the trees. When the Mosses left sooner than anticipated, Darrell used the cellular phone to call his boss. Two well-placed bribes at the harbormaster's office had ensured the Mosses' departure, although it wasn't expected quite so early.

Once alerted by Darrell, Bantam came out and parked in a secluded spot just north of Liebowitz's, a small cabin off the main highway owned by snowbirds. Everyone knew the owners flew south to their big house in California long before the snow came. They stayed for the June-July-August fishing, and when the fish emigrated, so did they.

After grunting his way along the four-wheeler trail Darrell had torn into the moss and ferns, J. T. found Darrell and together they waited for Smokey Joe Widdecomb to leave. The rig noise was great cover.

While waiting, they planned their next move. J. T. would go first. If unseen, he would use the blackjack and knock Jim

Bruno out. If seen, he would strike up a conversation with the pleasantly surprised Bruno, keeping him distracted until Darrell could sneak up and hit him from behind. If necessary, they would both hit him. Shooting was to be avoided if possible. This had to look like an accident, although they both had guns.

Their opportunity came when the witcher drove away. But before they got organized, Bruno hit water! Damn!

They knew they'd have to go after the bags of P-mix once the big driller was incapacitated. When J. T. saw the frothing water splash and Big Jim act like he just won the lottery, he knew they witnessed the strike. He also knew that Jim Bruno would be distracted, and he was right.

"C'mon, Goddammit! Move it!" Bantam scowled for emphasis. Darrell snapped out of his trance. He had been staring at the unconscious driller the way a snake looks at a bird's nest full of eggs. Before the next minute passed, he was gone.

The mayor wore his Neoprene fishing waders to keep dry going through the ferns. With the weather turning worse as it was, he was glad he had them on. The long pockets in front held G-B ties, the white plastic wire straps with an "eye" at one end, the "head." The other end slid through and ratcheted until it became tight. He'd used the smaller ones for wiring before, but if he hadn't seen a cop show on T.V. where they used them for handcuffs, he never would have thought of it.

Grunting every time he leaned over or squatted, Jake worked to uncover Big Jim's arm from beneath him. When the mayor freed it, Jim's face fell further into the mud. The shoulder that held his face up now reached behind him. Having both of Bruno's wrists together, J. T. reached into his front pocket, pulled out a tie and threaded it behind Jim's wrists. He then inserted the tip of the white plastic through the square on the opposite end. He pulled it through with a hard tug, letting go of Bruno's wrists at the same time. The zipper-sound was satisfying. He added another to Bruno's wrists then put two around his ankles. These things are great, he thought. No marks!

J. T. pulled, pushed and lifted until he had the big driller positioned the way he wanted. He took his eyes off Bruno for the first time to look for witnesses. They had tried to get Jim twice and missed. It would be a shame to be this close and have it spoiled by someone spotting them.

The first time they missed him was after Darrell had rigged the E-brake on Jim's old rig and he escaped unscathed. The second was when Ed was shocked by the welder. Darrell had melted the insulation off the welding machine's main feed with a small hand torch late at night. Unfortunately Ed, not Big Jim, had been the one hurt. Now, after today they both would be out of the picture. This well project would fail. Jake Bantam needed it to fail, and fail badly.

Satisfied there was no one watching, J. T. looked at the drill rig and its controls. Many years had passed since his doodle-bug days drilling shot holes. The seismographic exploration outfit he worked for used a different type rig, but he'd run a few cable tool rigs in his day. Grabbing the control for the bailer, he raised and lowered the tool a few times. Satisfied with his command of the bailer line, J. T. moved on to the main line control. Placing one hand on the clutch and the other on the brake, he pulled with the left while releasing the brake with the right. The bit came up. He lowered it, picked it up, lowered it. Pleased with his dexterity, he let the bit hang.

Soon Darrell was back with six bags of Ready-mix piled three high on the back of the four-wheeler. He maneuvered right up to the well and turned away. He ground the machine into reverse before stopping, then backed up next to the water well.

To Darrell's surprise, J. T. grabbed a bag of Ready-mix and tore it open. This type of work was normally reserved for Darrell. The paper dog-food-type bag held sand, gravel and a small plastic pouch of cement. Once mixed together with water the bag's contents would make concrete.

"All right! Throw the plastic bags in whole. Then pour in the sand and gravel! I'll mix 'em down hole with the bit."

Darrell nodded and did as ordered. He liked listening to the kerplunks and splashes echoing from far below.

While J. T. let the bit down to break open the plastic bags and mix the cement into concrete, Darrell looked down at the big driller, thinking, smart-ass guy doesn't look so tough all muddy, tied up on the wet ground. Always thought he was better than everybody else. Not now, huh? Darrell was eager to see what the big man's guts would look like after J. T. dropped the bit on him.

"Darrell!" Bantam snapped. "Goddammit! We gotta get outta here!" The mayor had the bit, now gray-colored from the concrete, back at the surface. He was waiting for Darrell to dump in another bag.

They repeated the process five more times. Once Jake was convinced, he raised the bit out of the hole. He began to bail. They used the water that came up in the bailer to clean the concrete from the bit and the area surrounding the well. No trace of cement was left. It took fifteen full bails to empty the well, but finally it did go dry—proof their cementing job worked. Unless someone drilled through the now-hardening concrete, no one would ever know Bruno hit water here.

The water splashing over him awakened Jim Bruno. Moaning and bleary-eyed, Big Jim was having trouble focusing. His head hurt like hell.

"Shit!" J. T. cursed his luck. It would have been much better if Bruno had remained unconscious.

"Want me to hit him again, boss?" Darrell begged.

"No! I don't want to risk marking him up if we don't have to."

Jim was regaining consciousness slowly, through a fog. At least he thought that was what he was doing. Once his brain and sense of sight synchronized again, he thought he must be dreaming or something. That could be the only explanation for seeing J. T. at the controls of his rig. That was the image he thought he saw, before he had to close his eyes tight to battle off a wave of headache pain that hit him as soon as he focused.

Jim got his eyes open again. He was disoriented. His hands tingled painfully as though asleep. His thoughts clustered together. He had mud on his face and his back was wet. The pain in his head was throbbing now, instead of continual.

Again he saw Jake Bantam at the controls of the rig. Something about him wasn't right. The mayor had on work clothes; gloves, hat and some type of fancy bibs. What the hell was going on here? Jim had never seen Jake Bantam so out of character. This bothered Jim. The mayor always wore dress slacks, the pockets bulging with keys and money.

There was something else Jim didn't like. There was a disturbing look on the mayor's face. Something in those brow-shrouded eyes. Something....

J T. pulled on the main line control and began raising the drill stem, not stopping, allowing it to climb.

Shit, Jim thought, he's going to crown out! Jim tried to get up and out from under the bit. He couldn't! What the Hell? Pulling on his hands, Jim realized he was tied up.

"What the hell is going on here, Theo?" Jim demanded.

Just short of hitting the mast crown with the top of the drill stem, J. T. stopped and set the brake. The bottom of the bit was over twenty feet off the ground, directly over Jim.

Jim had never looked at the bit from this viewpoint and it was making him very uncomfortable. He and Ed would never leave the stem up that high unless they were adding a particularly long section of casing. If they did, they wouldn't leave it up there for long. It made the derrick top heavy. If J. T. let the brake loose....

"What the Hell do you think you're doing, Jake?" Jim demanded again, pissed now, feeling violated.

"Killing you," Bantam answered, nonchalantly.

Big Jim's heart sank like a chunk of glacier ice calving off into the bay. What was planned became obvious.

A driller is always aware of the possibility he might sometime set the bit down on his foot. Of course they all strive to avoid it. But this was too much. Jim tried to kick at the mayor and his helper, wiggle himself free. Anything. But all he could do was barely move in a worm fashion. Not very devastating to his tormentors, one of whom was giggling while pulling a gun from his belt.

"He moves like that again, shoot him in the gut." Jake said, looking at the .38 in Darrell's hand.

Darrell nodded gleefully. "You got it boss."

Jim, exasperated now, was trying desperately to remember what, if anything, he had done to the mayor to warrant this.

"Kill me? What... Why?"

"It ain't nothing personal, Jimbo," J. T. grunted. "It's oil, boy. Lots of it."

"What?" Jim said, eyes darting from the drill stem high overhead to the shotgun, still leaning against the tree where he left it. There was no way he could get to it without first freeing his hands. Maybe he could roll, just as J. T. released the brake. J. T. would be looking up as he began dropping the stem. Then what? Darrell looked eager to shoot him.

"You really didn't think some ski-mo ghost blew up your old rig on the way to Ninilchik, did you? Mmmnpphh..." J. T. paused to dig his lighter out from the deep pocket in his bibs. He clicked it and lit the cigarette in the holder he'd been clenching in the corner of his mouth since Darrell called him. After drawing deeply to bring it to life, he smiled. The bastard was clearly enjoying this.

"In sixty-eight I worked pushing the seis crew that surveyed this 640 acres and the 640 acre homestead next door." He pointed north. "The reflections were good. Very good. In fact, they showed a huge reservoir, likely over a million barrels at 6,000 feet to 7,000 feet. Not near as deep or expensive to get to as drilling in Prudhoe Bay is. The surrounding areas showed small reservoir pockets, not enough on their own to be profitable." He paused to moan out a grunt. "Mmmmmph."

"Somehow those charts were misplaced and then ended up exchanged with dummy charts of two sections that showed nothing." J. T. sucked on his cigarette holder, then held it out to look at it while exhaling blue smoke. "Being the best find in Alaska besides Prudhoe, I'm certain that Rampart Oil will want to drill here once someone points out this grievous error in record keeping." The mayor smiled, proud of his cunning.

"Of course, I will be happy to point out this mistake. That is, once I own the mineral rights to both 640 acre parcels."

"You have to kill me to get the mineral rights to this place? Why? I don't have them!"

J. T., pleased that Jim still hadn't figured out his ingenious plan, puffed twice more on his cigarette. If Jim couldn't see it, it was doubtful anyone else would. He took the nasty-looking tar-stained holder out of his mouth, rolled it back and forth in his fingers, eying it as though he were considering having it for lunch.

"Course you don't! The state has 'em! I suppose you were too worried about all these monsters running around here to think about much else, eh?" He paused deliberately to look at Darrell and grin unnaturally. "You musta forgot that the Department of Resources requires that to obtain a drilling permit the mineral rights must be owned by the applicant. The only way to own mineral rights is to own a complete original 640 acre homestead without having sold off any part of it. If the 640 isn't owned in one section like the section I own next to here, then the state takes ownership of the rights. For the good of the people, you understand. You wouldn't want some backwoods chicken-plucker like Moss getting upset 'cause a big rig set up and started drilling for oil next door, now, would ya?" J. T. smiled that sickening smile again. "But you already knew all that, huh Jimbo?"

Yes, Goddammit, Jim thought.

"You're doing all this for money?" Jim asked, afraid of the answer.

"Not money boy, millions! I'm doing this to get the hell out of this ungrateful shithole of a town," the portentous bald man said. "Head down to Vegas! Now there's a real town!

"When that old bastard Thompson sold this twenty acres to Moss it set me back a few years. I've been working on this a long time, Bud. Now with the Mosses so depressed about this dry hole, and you getting killed by ghosts and all, I imagine I just might be able to buy this place. Pretty cheap too, I bet!" J. T. and Darrell chuckled together.

It was sinking in now. These two were the reason Ed was in the hospital, and the reason he would be dead soon if he didn't do something. Rage was filling Big Jim like steam in a pressure cooker, but there was no vent. He twisted and worked his hands against the ties. If he could just get his hands on the shotgun. Or on Darrell...

"Mmmmmmpphhhh... You really thought the Devil blew up your rig and then shocked your helper, didn't cha? Ha! I even had ol' Darrell, 'the spook,' here dump a fifty-pound sack of rock salt down the community well. Curiously enough, that well will miraculously clear up with your demise and stoppage of work out here at Moss's. That salt should just about be pumped out of there by now!"

Jim was burning now. He had bought all of it. He strained to look toward the driveway. Shit, he should've had Sam stay and just sent Annie in.

"Don't be thinking the Mosses are coming to save you. We're keeping them busy in town. Yep. Darrell's been a real busy spook here lately."

Bruno glanced fractionally up at the bit hanging over him like a guillotine. The sprinkles had turned to rain, stinging his eyes. He had to look away. He did *not* want to die like this!

"Did you pay Ezra Jacobson to murder his own brother, too?" Jim already knew the answer to that question. He needed to stall for time. Time to get his hands free.

"Naw. But it got me thinking. I was standing in the mercantile office, looking out at all that brown shit coming down. I thought about what had happened to Arn the day before, and it hit me." J. T.'s chest swelled with pride. He looked disappointed that Jim wasn't showing more appreciation. "With them ski-mo caves out there, I figgered we could work it so there'd be so many ghosts running around here misbehaving that nobody but me would want to buy this place once they do try to sell. Hell, I'm sure they'll thank me for taking it off their hands! Ha!"

"And everybody will just say how lucky you are when Rampart decides to drill here huh?" Jim asked, hating to admit the mayor's plan looked tight, solid.

"That's right, Jimbo." The mayor's voice had gone serious now. His hand was back on the brake.

"What about Percy Leibowitz? Darrell kill him too?"

J. T. looked at Darrell who simply shrugged in ignorance. "What about him?" Bantam seemed genuinely surprised.

"He was killed yesterday. Supposedly by a moose."

"Bullshit. You're just trying to stall."

As he began to release the brake, J. T.'s chest exploded outward with a loud whack!

Jim's face was dank now. Blood spattered onto him. Was that a gunshot?

The mayor's body jolted. Legs buckling, he dropped straight down on his knees.

J. T.'s hand grabbed for the brake in an effort to stay up. When he fell over on his side, dead, his hand released the brake inadvertently.

The drill stem was free-falling.

The sound of the main reel spinning snapped Jim out of astonishment and into response. Big Jim did an ungainly looking backward somersault.

Halfway through the roll, he heard and felt a powerful thud right behind the back of his neck.

Jim ended up on his stomach unable to move because of the cuttings trough. He lay face down in the mud, looking at the bottom of the drill stem. The bit was buried three feet into the soft mossy ground. On the other side of the stem lay the "General." What little Jim could see of him was motionless.

Twisting his neck against his shoulders and still-bound arms, Jim tried to get a look at Darrell Klepesen. He was trying to find out what the hell just happened. He was also worried Darrell was going to shoot him.

Jim could just barely see Darrell crouching, pointing the .38 toward the driveway. It looked as if he were trying to determine where the shot that killed his boss originated. The look on Darrell's sheep-dog face indicated he was as confused as Bruno.

"Drop it 'cha worm!"

Jim knew that voice.

Darrell zeroed in on the voice. It came from a gray-haired Grizzly Adams look-alike who was leaning over the hood of Jim Bruno's tool truck, leveling a rifle directly at him with one eye closed.

Fido Tasker.

Darrell dropped the handgun and held both bands out, open, without being told. Big Jim could see the repugnant smile had vanished from his pockmarked face.

The momentum of the free-falling drill stem caused the main reel to continue spinning. The brake hadn't been set. The cable was bird nested around the draw works like an abused fishing reel. Even though it was stuck in the ground, the top was not being held by any tension. The drill stem began to topple. Starting very slowly, it was falling directly toward Jim, and Darrell wasn't making any moves to help him.

All Jim could do was worm-crawl under the back of the rig, pushing himself along with his toes. The more the stem leaned, the more it picked up speed.

Jim didn't make it all the way under.

The bit end uprooted itself as the rope-socket at the top came down, nearly meeting the ground.

Jim expected pain.

When the bit portion of the stem first laid across his legs protruding from the back of the rig, he should have been hurt. Surprisingly, he wasn't. Just weight; a lot of weight pressing down on the backs of his thighs. He tried to turn and get out from under it.

When he did, the top of the stem hit the ground. The bit end was lifted for an instant, then came snapping back onto Jim's leg with a wicked reverberation.

"Aaahhhhh!" Jim yelled in pain. Something in his leg gave.

"Jimmy! You all right son?" Jim heard that wonderful old craggly voice again. Fido sounded concerned. He was yelling to be heard over the rig engine noise.

"I... ah... yeah. Yeah I'm okay Fido. Think my leg is broke or something though."

"Cut him loose, now!" Fido said to Darrell, deadly serious. "Then toss the knife down the hill."

Feeling his hands being freed was wonderful. God, it felt good to be able to use them again! The first thing he did was put both hands down and lift his face up out of the mud. Then he wiped the rainwater, blood and sweat from his cheeks and forehead.

Damn! His leg hurt like hell. His head hurt like hell. He could almost drag himself out from under the bit, but not quite.

"Fido! Can you get this son-of-a-bitch off me?" Jim panted, "I can't get out!"

"Hang on a sec, Jimmy!" Fido yelled at Darrell, "Hug that tree, worm!"

Fido must have gotten a pry bar under the stem. Jim felt the pressure on his leg decrease. Using his arms Jim dragged himself from under the stem, pushing with his good leg, the injured leg dragging along uselessly. Jim kept going until he came out under the welder. Fido and that big beautiful gray beard were there to greet him.

"Jimmy! You look like shit, son," Fido Tasker said to his protege, grinning broadly. To Jim, Fido never looked so good.

"They bushwhacked me, Fido. I never saw them coming," Jim said embarrassed, rubbing the back of his head.

"Can you stand, Jimmy?" Fido asked, placing a hand under Jim's arm. Jim was surprised how strong the veteran driller still was. While lifting Jim with one hand, the other hand held the .38, which was aimed in the general direction of Darrell Klepesen. Darrell stood with his arms around a medium-size spruce tree just to the back of the well.

Jim groaned his way to his feet with Fido's help. He leaned against the rig's catwalk, favoring his bum leg. It hurt bad. The piercing ache was almost too much. He was covered with mud nearly head to toe.

"Ain't that J. T. Bantam?" Fido asked him, pointing the .38 in the corpse's direction.

Jim nodded yes.

"Who inna hell pissed in his corn flakes?"

Jim just shook his head imperceptibly. He wasn't sure he really understood it well enough to explain why this happened.

"I believe he meant to kill you, Jimmy. I was watching for quite a spell. They didn't hear me come in on account a' I got me a new muffler on the pickup. I parked a little ways off trying to surprise you. Good thing it's moose season or I wouldn't of had the .30-06 with me. I didn't want to kill 'um, Jimmy, I waited as long as I could. It looked like he meant t' shish-ke-bob ya, Jimmy!" Fido was rambling a bit more than usual, even for him. Jim could tell Mr. Tasker's adrenaline was pumping.

"What the hell's going on here anyway? I heard about your helper getting hurt on the radio. When you didn't answer your phone I gave that crazy dog-face bastard Jester a call. He said your welder was fubb'ed, so I brought you a loaner."

"Fubbed?" Jim thought he knew all Jester's terminology. Fido did, having also been a "dog face" in Korea. For some reason, he had to ask.

"Yeah, fucked up beyond belief."

"So what's this all about? I know a dry hole will piss people off, but Jesus Kee-rist!"

"I got water, Fido, lots of it." Jim answered flatly. Reluctantly he looked at J. T.'s body.

Blood was oozing out both the entry and exit wounds. Bruno expected to see a look of shock, indignation or similar emotion on the face of the dead man. Curiously, a look of bliss had taken up permanent residence. It was a look Jim had never seen on the "General" before. He appeared happy, oblivious to the rain accumulating on his face.

Looking at the man, Jim thought to himself that J. T. had crossed the two biggest lines of all: the line separating good from evil and the line separating life from death.

What does it take for a man to cross a line so big and become evil? What causes a person to go so wrong that he feels no remorse for the pain and suffering he causes his fellow man? Money? Was simple greed enough to do it? Wrestling with his mind, Jim couldn't come up with the answer.

"Jimmy! Can you walk? You all right, son?" Fido's voice snapped him out of it. Jim realized he'd been gazing fixedly at the dead ex-mayor.

"Huh? Yeah, I think so, Fido. Hurts like hell though." Jim grimaced, looking down at his thigh, gauging it over with his hand. "You saved my ass again, Fido. Thanks."

"Don't mention it, I mean to anybody. Most folks won't hire contractors that shoot customers first and ask questions later." Turning serious, he said, "Jimmy, we need to get to a phone and call the troopers about this. Before we do, can you tell me why did I have to shoot this here bald guy?" Again pointing the .38 at J. T., Fido was understandably puzzled why Jake Bantam tried to kill his buddy Jim Bruno.

"Oil, Fido. Lots and lots of oil."

Right then you could have taken a picture of Fido Tasker's face and used it for the symbol of the international question mark.

Jim sighed and looked down at J. T. again. This could take a while to explain.

CHAPTER THIRTY-TWO

John T. Webb enjoyed his job this afternoon. He always did.

He liked the way the muscles and tendons in his forearms flexed and bulged whenever he changed course, turning the big steering wheel or switching gears with the three-foot high shifter.

Webb got a thrill controlling the power, the force, the sheer bulk. The momentum involved in the load behind him. The knowledge of the damage it could do if he made a mistake, especially today.

He enjoyed watching the trailer swing left and then back right past the back of the cab on slow, big turns. He liked the sounds too. The engine noise when the R.P.M.'s topped out, catching up to the throttle pedal. The hhssssstt of released air when the foot application pedal was set free. The braaap braaap braaap the Jacob's compression release brake made when switched on. Rubber humming loudly under him in eighteen different places indicating all was well.

John liked the heated external mirrors that deiced themselves, his air-adjustable seat, the rows of switches across the dashboard, like a 747. He liked looking back at the shiny stainless-steel tanker and seeing everything he passed reflected back in fun-house-mirror fashion.

Webb loved his job. If he ever did finally get "monied-up," John Webb would continue to drive truck, though maybe not quite as much.

Looking briefly away from the road to the dash-mounted clocks behind the steering wheel, John smiled. Ahead of schedule again. He'd be pulling into the fuel terminal on the Homer Spit in forty minutes.

CHAPTER THIRTY-THREE

Jim held the .38 on Darrell Klepesen while Fido went inside Moss's cabin. He placed a call to the troopers, then rummaged for aspirin or anything that would help Big Jim stave off the pain in his leg. The trooper's response time would give them plenty of window to get the story straight.

Fido emerged quickly with a partially consumed pint of brandy and a bottle of Advil. Jim swapped the gun for the pills and brandy, then consumed a healthy portion of each.

Fearing the pain that might be involved with unnecessary movements, Jim chose to remain standing. He began explaining to Fido what he knew about J. T.'s motives. Roughly halfway through, Jim noticed the empty bags of P-mix on the four-wheeler. He looked at Darrell, who was still hugging the spruce tree. It would have been comical had the situation not been so grave.

Glowering indignantly, Jim pointed to the bags, and asked Darrell, "Did you pour those in?"

Darrell simply changed his expression back to the slanted grin he had been showing earlier.

"Shit!" Jim knew that drilling out a chunk of concrete that size could take days.

"Hey, Jimmy! If I drill on that sum'bitch now, it won't a' set up yet!" Fido beamed, grinning that wide grin at his friend once more.

POW!

A tremendous earsplitting snap boomed at them from the other side of the rig. All three men ducked their heads in reaction. They looked up to find out where the sound of cracking timber originated. It was unmistakably wood being torn, broken.

A tree was falling. Before Fido and Jim could react, its top crossed over the rig's draw works with a loud swish of branches, needles and pine cones showering in all directions.

POW!

Another tree was falling, this time on their side of the rig.

CRAAACK! POW!

This tree was falling right at them. When the trunk was at a forty-five degree angle it let out another loud popping crack. The severed wood at the tree's base twisted, spinning it away from Jim and Fido just enough to miss them.

What the hell? Jim thought. The weather was still deteriorating, rain coming down constantly harder, the wind was blowing more now, but there had been no lightning strikes, no thunder.

POW! POW!

Two more trees cracked at the base and were falling in their direction. The trees would not reach them, but the way they were all falling in their direction was just too weird.

Darrell already opted to let go of the tree he'd been hugging. He was looking at it, apparently trying to decide if it were going to pop next. He couldn't decide whether to shit or go blind. Agape, as were the two men detaining him, he looked at Fido who was still holding a gun on him. Then he looked at the downed trees. Darrell looked again at the men, and bolted.

The bushy-gray-haired man halfway raised the gun toward Darrel's wake then stopped, thinking better of it.

"Why hell, we'll let the troopers worry about him. Saves us havin' to watch the worm," Fido reasoned.

Jim was relieved Fido hadn't fired at Darrell.

The two friends looked at the trees, then to each other for an explanation. Fido shrugged his shoulders.

"Come on partner, let's get you to a..."

Darrell nearly reached the trees at the end of the clearing around Moss's cabin, a good seventy-five yards away, when he let out a horrified wail.

What Jim Bruno saw was astonishing.

The beast looked like a very large skeletal Jack Russell that was overdosed on steroids and PCP. Vicious, standing at least four feet high, it was postured to attack Darrell. Some mangy- looking flesh clung to its back, ribs and hindquarters, like a blanket thrown over a horse. For the most part, the animal's legs and head were bone. Its jaw was open, baring what seemed like hundreds of teeth. There was something about the eyes....

The creature lunged at Darrell, charging through his arms held up in defense, unaffected. It took Darrell down by the throat, cutting his scream short.

Fido looked at Jim in disbelief. Jim could only answer by nodding at the .38 in Fido's hand.

Hurriedly, Fido gave the handgun over to Jim. He went for the .30-06 that lay on the rig's catwalk.

Fido clicked off the safety. He had previously ejected the shell from the round that killed J. T.; a fresh round was already in the chamber.

Shouldering the rifle, Fido took aim.

The creature was savagely chewing at Darrell Klepesen's neck. Darrell was not moving. Fido fired.

"Goddamn!"

"You hit 'um Fido?"

"Thought I did! What kinda varmit issat?"

Fido chambered another round, aimed and fired.

This time they both saw it. The bullet struck the animal in the ribs. Bone fragments ricocheted on impact. The bullet did not affect the animal in the least. It continued to gnaw at Darrell.

The dog-thing lifted its head and stared directly at the men, jaw open, ringed with Darrel's blood. The eyes. Jim recognized them. He had seen them before.

In Alton's classroom.

Those eyes. Dark, glowing red and empty. Empty except for one emotion. Hate.

This thing was pure evil. It was the kikituk. Or shaman. Or both. Had to be.

"This isn't fair! The picture showed it to only be eighteen inches tall!" Jim complained to himself.

In the past Bruno used his size to his advantage, the way a pretty girl uses her smile. It got him quick respect in situations where he might have had to otherwise earn it first. But it was quite clear this monster, looking directly at them, didn't give a shit how big Jim was. His size wasn't even being considered.

There was another loud POW! The tree Darrell had been hugging exploded at the base and was popping and cracking toward them violently.

Fido quickly looked at Jim's bum leg and then at Jim. Thinking along the same lines, they interlocked shoulders. With the tree coming down behind them, they worked their way to the front of the rig, Jim moving like an injured football player leaving the game.

The upper portion of the tree hit Fido on the right shoulder, causing him to stumble but not hitting him hard enough to put him down. It did cause him to drop the rifle.

"Jimmy, I think we ought to leave now."

"You don't have to ask me twice, Fido. Grab the shotgun in case that thing gets close, wouldja?"

"What for? You saw I hit that ... that. ..whatever-the-hell-it-is both times!"

Fido made sure Jim was balanced well enough to keep from falling over, then went back and grabbed Moss's shotgun.

Jim felt strange evacuating without first shutting down the rig.

Shotgun in one hand, Jim Bruno in the other, Fido began making his way to the truck. Looking down at their feet while moving, Fido said, "I did hit that varmit, Jimmy."

Jim had been moose hunting with Fido many times. He never missed.

They nearly reached Fido's truck when the pair was alerted to a vehicle's approach by the rattle-trap noise it made. Jim heard the sound of its muffler bottoming-out a time or two before. Once in view, Jim's suspicions were confirmed. It was, of course, Roy Patterson in his M. V., driving into the wrong place at the wrong time.

Fido got Jim leaned into the truck's quarter panel. He opened the passenger door. Before Jim got in, both men took a peek to see where the monster was.

It heard the M. V. coming also. It watched them as Roy-Boy was pulling in. Then it charged.

"Shit!" Jim said loudly. Hurrying into the truck, he yelped in pain, bumping his leg.

Fido ran around the front of the pick-up with one of his big hands on the hood for balance. Fido got in. Luckily, the truck started on the first try.

Roy Patterson pulled in and stopped. Before shutting his engine down he saw the kikituk coming at him, snarling murderously. It looked ghastly.

Roy-Boy put the M. V. in reverse, backed up a short distance, then stopped.

"What the FUCK is that hippie doing?" Fido yelled, impatient, waiting for Roy-Boy to get out of the way so he could back up and get turned around to leave. Just before the growling Kikituk reached the Mosses' parking area, Roy-Boy gassed the M. V.

Tires spinning, gravel flying out from under the back wheels, Roy Patterson was heading for a head-on with a hell hound. The malevolent creature was snarling, coming straight for Roy, with teeth gnashing.

As Jim realized what Roy-Boy was planning, a recollection of two Dall sheep lowering their heads for battle came into his bewildered mind.

The monster did not slow.

Neither did Roy.

BLAM!

The collision was severe.

The amazing thing was that the M. V. was stopped cold, as if it had struck a tree. Roy-Boy was thrown forward into the steering wheel. Steam rose from the collapsed front of the vehicle, now hissing in pain.

The Kikituk was knocked off its feet but was struggling to get up. It had not been knocked far from the collision, and it was grunting angrily.

Fido backed up, got turned around, pointed the truck out, then rolled down his window to yell. "C'mon, hippie!"

Roy-Boy shoved his shoulder into his door to force it open. He got out clutching his chest, bent over slightly.

Jim opened the door for him, sliding over painfully, Shotgun in hand.

Roy got in, eyes wide. "What the hell is that? Cujo's wicked step-brother?"

They didn't have an answer for him.

Fido punched it. "You all right, son?" Tasker asked him, respect coming through his voice in appreciation for what Roy-Boy did.

"My chest hurts," he said, rubbing the affected area. "But, yeah, I'm okay."

Fido took a look in his rear-view mirror. He grumbled, "I don't believe this shit." Big Jim and Roy-Boy both turned around. Not only was the Kikituk on its feet, but it was chasing them.

And gaining.

The gravel road's condition and all the turns limited Fido's ability to increase his speed and the Kikituk was remarkably fast. Fido gained ground on the straightaways then lost it while slowing for a corner. At this rate, it would catch up to them very soon.

Jim was torn between watching which one would kill them first: Fido's driving or the freak of nature on their tail. Looking from front to rear, Jim could see the snarling ugly creature that had gore and human blood foaming around its mouth. His anxiety increased. Roy-Boy did not look happy either.

"Look out!" Roy screamed.

A birch tree up ahead was beginning to fall across the road in front of them. Its wide span made it appear far more formidable than the falling spruce trees had been.

Fido cranked hard left on the steering wheel, driving halfway in the ditch, halfway on the road's shoulder.

The top third of the tree hit the truck in a crash of branches and metal. As Fido drove through, the right side mirror was ripped-off by a thick branch. It made a hard sounding clunk, then rattled down along the bed. Glass imploded into the cab on Roy-Boy's side as well as another branch of the tree. This one sliced Roy's forehead.

The truck fishtailed sideways, throwing Roy-Boy into Jim, Jim into Fido. Fido recovered, straightened out and stepped on the gas pedal again. All three looked back. They saw the vampire-dog clear the trunk of the tree and continue its pursuit. It had just gained ground.

It was right on their ass.

The highway was ahead now, within view.

"It's about to jump in the back!" Roy squealed.

Highway coming closer, Fido showed no intention of letting off the gas and applying some brakes for the ninety-degree turn he would have to make up ahead.

Jim looked at the approaching highway, then he looked at Fido's eyes.

Fido's eyes were darting back and forth, from the northern part of the highway, to the road directly in front of them.

When Jim turned his head north to see what Fido was looking at, he couldn't believe it. A shiny, stainless-steel gasoline tanker southbound at full speed.

Jim instantly recognized what Fido was planning. He was gauging, speculating, measuring. Risking their lives.

"No way, Fido!" Jim yelled over the lively, creaking noise of the pick-up. The Kikituk had him scared shitless, but now he was about to freak.

"Drop yer cocks and grab yer socks, boys! We're gonna get western with this son-of-a-bitch!"

The second before they were to be T-boned by an eighteen-wheeler, Jim and Roy both put their hands on the dash and tucked their heads into their shoulders like a couple of turtles. They yelled, the kind of scream a guy lets go when he thinks he is about to die.

Fido yelled also. "YEE-HAH!"

An air horn went off, blasting vehement protest. The three men in the pickup crossed the highway.

Jim pinched his eyes closed. He felt the truck's tires go airborne as they reached the pavement. His stomach rolled over when his brain recognized the vehicle his body was traveling in was out of control. The air horn to their immediate right was very loud now, blasting in where the passenger's window used to be.

BASH!

The sickening sound of meat impacting metal followed them to their crash-landing. The semi's horn was silent.

They survived the fuel truck. Its rear twelve tires were now locked up and skidding, leaving smoking black stripes on the highway behind them.

Fido had timed it right. Now they just needed to survive stopping.

The pickup hit hard, bouncing down over the highway's shoulder opposite Moss's road. Into the dying fireweed they went, all three of them hitting their heads on the cab's ceiling when the truck hit the second time. Once through the fireweed lining the road's right-of-way, Fido's pickup hit the alders.

The alder trees provided a buffer for the spruce beginning at the right-of-way's end. Alders are great for smoking fish, custom woodworking, teepee poles, or fence stakes.

They are not good to drive into.

When John Webb looked back up from checking the time, movement from a frontage road caught his peripheral attention. The pickup was going *way too fast!* It wasn't going to stop in time!

To his credit, John Webb threw the trailer brake lever and then laid on the horn while gently applying the tractor brakes. This would avoid a jackknife and provide the maximum deceleration possible. The trucker's rectum puckered when he saw the pickup leave the frontage road on a collision course with his rig. He was about to kill the people in that truck.

Something was behind them. It... it looked like an extremely large dog with a very bad case of mange.

Webb braced for the impending collision.

The pickup made it by, but he hit the dog with a nasty-sounding bash!

John Webb downshifted, preparing to stop. He would have to check his radiator for damage and see if those crazy bastards in the pick-up were all right.

As he released the trailer brake John Webb got the scare of his life.

He got a glimpse of what he just hit when it looked over the hood of the Kenworth at him.

It wasn't dead! Jesus, Mary, and Joseph!

The mostly fleshless skull and blood-covered jaw that shrieked at him startled the poor truck driver so bad he stood on the brake, slowing the tractor but doing little to slow the fully loaded trailer behind him. The tanker began to come around, and on the gradual corner he was coming into, he had no choice but to hang on and ditch.

The thing on the hood was clawing to stay on, to get at him. But when the big rig left the highway, it disappeared underneath.

Yes, I am worried now, was what John was thinking as the kinked tractor-trailer came to a stop in the ditch. At least a minute ago, he knew where the thing was. Should I get out? he wondered.

A look in his mirror answered the question. The tank had ruptured.

Motionless, and glad to be that way, Fido, Jim and Roy-Boy looked at each other cautiously. Roy was bleeding from the gash on his forehead, blood running down both sides of his nose.

"Oh yeah! Run the bastard right into the grille! Pretty good huh?" Fido claimed proudly.

"Goddammit, Fido! You scared the shit outta me!" Jim said crossly.

"Hoo-boy! Kinda got my heart pumpin' too!" Fido said, grinning at his injured passengers. "Well drilling ain't for weenies, is it, Jimbo?"

Bruno had to laugh out loud. This was what Fido used to say all the time when Jim worked for him. He'd say it when things with a particular job weren't going well, or if the weather sucked, or if they ran out of beer.

Once convinced they were still alive, Jim relented, having had a few seconds to catch his breath and think.

"Thanks, Fido. You did good."

"Sure. Anytime you need a ride, just let me know. I'll send somebody else." They needed to get out and see what happened to the fuel truck and its driver. It sounded as if he had gone off the road big time.

Fido tried to start the pickup. It turned for half a revolution then locked up. Fido gave a sideways glance and then got out.

"Awwww shit!" he said, complaining loudly when he got a look at the damage.

The alders perforated the truck's front half. The left front tire was flat. The hood and fenders were trashed. Several large alder poles ran up into the engine, most likely into the fan, radiator and oil pan since antifreeze and engine oil were all over the place. So much for the new muffler.

Roy's door wouldn't open. He climbed through where the window had been. Big Jim starting sliding out Fido's side, not noticing any pain in his leg.

"Jimmy, hand me that shotgun, willya, Bud?"

Jim looked at Fido in disbelief. "Fido, you don't think..."

"No I... Hell I don't know what to think. I never seen nothin' like that varmint." He reached out, waiting for Jim to hand him the scatter gun.

Jim did so grudgingly.

Fido and Roy helped Jim out of the ditch, onto the highway. They saw the tractor-trailer about 200 yards down the road. It was in the ditch on the opposite side. They moved tentatively. Fido had put a scare back into them.

At 100 yards away they could see the driver was out of the semi. Fluid was pouring out of a crinkle in the tanker. The driver had a fire extinguisher and was spraying it... but not on the fire that was beginning to consume the engine. He was spraying it underneath the cab of the tractor; spraying it on something that was thrashing and screeching at him wildly.

The three men looked at each other as if to say, Are you seeing this too? Unbelievable. The kikituk was still alive.

"Brother are we in trouble." Fido said, looking down at the shotgun in his hand that might as well be a pea-shooter. "That thing can really take a punch!"

Not wanting to get any closer, but wanting to help the truck driver they brought into this mess, the men inched their way toward the cacophony ahead. Suddenly the truck driver threw the fire extinguisher and ran, coming toward them.

He was flailing his arms. Yelling something.

"Get back! Go on! Get away!" He was shouting desperately at them. "It's gonna...."

KA-BOOM!

The entire trailer concussed, shook and then turned into a scaled-down version of a nuclear explosion. The truck driver was knocked down. Even at their distance, the three could feel the heat.

As the fireball rose over the tops of the spruce trees, an extended primeval squall bellowed up in frustration within the flames.

186

Yaku now belonged to Shurok. The three men stared in awe.

"That Cujo bastard isn't gonna come out of those flames like some kind of *Terminator* puppy, is it, Big Jim?"

Jim and Fido looked at each other. Who knew?

"Let's get that driver on his feet 'n' ask him if he got a good look at that big ol' brown bear that ate that worm back at the job site, then chased us out here 'til he hit it!"

"Brown bear?" Jim and Roy both asked, looking at each other with wrinkled brows.

"Yeah!" Fido replied emphatically. "That bald sumbitch Bantam tried to kill Jim. I shot 'um, the bear came, ate that worm helper of Bantam,'s an' then chased us out here. Then this here trucker run that bear over an' crashed—is all what happened."

"They're never going to buy that, Fido," said Jim

"You think they have a choice?"

Fido was right, as usual. They couldn't exactly tell the troopers and everyone else that they'd been chased by a three-hundred-year-old shaman-dog.

An angry grizzly on his way to hibernation was, on the other hand, believable.

Fido left Jim leaning heavily on the undersized Roy-Boy to see if the truck driver was injured. Tasker helped the man to his feet. The trucker had skinned knees visible through the new holes in his pant legs. The palms of his hands retained some gravel. He seemed shaken, but otherwise in one piece. Which was very good if you compared his condition to that of his truck. The tractor-trailer, completely consumed, continued to burn, hiss, and pop as tires and air tanks took turns exploding.

The four men were in a huddle. The trucker introduced himself. His name was John Webb. He lived in Palmer close to the state fairgrounds, had done so for the last seventeen years. He seemed like a regular Joe. Mr. Webb wanted to know what the hell just happened.

The trucker held a graveled palm up to eye level and began plucking the tiny pebbles out of his hand. "What the hell was that thing?" he demanded.

Jim thought he recognized the accent. North Dakota, Minnesota probably. The trucker's head was Nordic in appearance, as were his shrouded eyes and jutting chin.

Jim and Roy-Boy looked sheepishly at each other, unable to answer him, until Fido bailed them out.

"That was the most pissed off grizzly bear you ever did run across! Er.. over. Man! Thanks for saving us! You got insurance, right?"

The trucker looked at Fido appraisingly.

"Grizzly bear," The trucker said flatly.

Fido was nodding his head slowly when he began another oration.

"Yeah! That snarlin' sumbitch chased us all the out to the highway! It was right on our ass! Good thing for us you came along when you did! Smashed 'um!"

Surprisingly calm, John Webb looked slowly away from the meaty part of his palm, most of the gravel removed now. His eyes met those of the gray-haired driller from Soldotna, and John Webb said, "That wasn't no bear that lived through getting crashed into, run over, stuck under my truck and then screamed at me like it did."

"Okay, what was it then?" Fido challenged sympathetically.

The trucker returned his gaze to his hand as if looking for more rocks. He brushed it, bent down, rubbed his knees briefly. He looked at all three conspirators, their expectant faces waiting, and said, "Yeah, that big mean ol' bear musta had rabies or something."

A concert of relief exhaled from the group. It was essential that their stories jive for the authorities. The truck driver was an intrinsic part of their credibility.

With that settled, Fido took over. He described to them what they would say to the troopers individually as well as together. He made them rehearse it a few times.

Gawkers were beginning to stop and congregate. Before he dispatched Roy-Boy to go home and call the troopers, Fido instructed Roy on exactly what to say and how to say it. Then Roy-Boy was gone.

Jim had to sit down awkwardly. His injured leg was stuck out like that of a fallen toy soldier. Fido took the truck driver aside and after a couple of minutes they were sharing mutual acquaintances from their respective towns. Soon Fido motioned the driver to sit down next to Bruno, while he went on to direct traffic.

Good ol' Fido, saving Jim's ass again, handling all this. Long after Jim went to the hospital, Fido would probably still be here explaining. Jim was lucky to have him.

The two of them sat watching the fire spread, watching Fido yell at the passersby stopping in the middle of the road to gawk. Their adrenaline started to subside.

As if sloshed in the face with a cocktail unexpectedly, Jim remembered. The OSHA investigators were supposed to be coming today! Shit! If they were to show up now and see all this destruction, talk about safety violations. Oh, brother! Not only will they fine him and pull his license for about ninety-nine years, they would probably put him in jail and throw the key down a well.

Hold it. Wait a minute.

He wasn't thinking rationally. Maybe he was going into shock or something. None of this was his fault, was it?

No.

They could not blame him for J. T.'s actions. Nor could he be held accountable for a "crazed, rabid grizzly bear" attacking Darrell and then chasing them out to the highway.

Jim noticed with a wince the pain in his leg was becoming much worse. Suddenly, he was very tired.

CHAPTER THIRTY-FOUR

J im awoke momentarily disorientated, but even though it was dark out, right away the sense of a sterile, antiseptic cleanliness told him he was in a hospital room.

His leg was very heavy. It seemed the right cheek of his butt was right up against some plaster. He struggled to get up, scooting himself onto the propped pillows at the top of the strange bed.

Blinking his eyes into focus, Jim heard a familiar voice. "Howdy, boss."

When Jim was brought in, Dr. White instructed the nurses to place him in the same room with Ed.

Jim smiled hello to his friend. He couldn't prevent his eyes from looking at the conspicuous vacancy next to Ed's remaining foot.

"Couple of cripples, ain't we?"

Bruno had to agree. Anchor Point Drilling was looking pretty beat-up about now; paralytic even.

Nodding at Ed's amputation, Jim queried him. "Hurt like hell, huh?"

"Uh-huh. Dr. Dan's giving me the best drugs in the house, though. It's not real bad until they start to wear off."

Jim's heart sank. "Man, Ed, I'm really sorry."

"Not your fault. I guess if it wasn't for Annie, I wouldn't be here."

Ed was surrounded. Balloons, magazines, books, and flowers decorated his side of the room. Jim was racked by more guilt for not sending some chocolates or something.

"Your mom?" Jim asked, looking at a balloon that had a Care Bear on it that said, "I can tell — You'll get well."

"Yeah," Ed said sheepishly.

Shit! He doesn't know! Hell, maybe nobody knows! Jim remembered.

"Hey! I hit the big water at Moss's today! Couldn't bail it down! Got a static at a hundred feet!"

Ed beamed. The news perked him up considerably.

"All right! So what all the hell happened out there today, boss? Fido shot J. T. and Darrell? Is Darrell the one that got me shocked?" Ed was like a dam about to burst with curiosity.

"Fido shot J. T., but not Darrell Klepesen." Ed was astonished.

Jim proceeded to tell Ed the whole story, interrupted only by a nurse occasionally checking in on the two broken-down drillers.

Fascinated, rapt with the tale, Jim could tell Ed wished he had been there despite the danger.

"So, is this monster-dog gone for good?"

"Man, I don't know." I wish you hadn't asked, thought Jim, adjusting his casted leg. The door burst open.

"Howdy boys! Damn, Jimmy! We wrecked two pickups, a semi, dropped some trees on top a everything and killed some bad guys! I'll bet if we'd a had better equipment we coulda done more damage, huh?"

Fido.

The door opened quickly once more. A nurse was on Fido's tail. She sternly began explaining to him he would have to leave and return once visiting hours began. Of course, Fido would have none of it.

"Honey, you bring your boss in here and have him try to throw me out, okay?"

She glowered at him, and gave Ed a small cupful of pills and watched as he swallowed, then she stormed out, contemptuous.

"Hiya, Eddie! How you feelin'?" He asked Ed enthusiastically.

"I'm okay." Ed was grinning broadly. He loved it.

Fido went on in his usual animated fashion about how it had taken all afternoon and a good part of the evening before investigators from the Alaska State Troopers were convinced. The appearance of a "rabid" brown bear of which no trace remained right after Fido shot J. T. Bantam was coincidence, nothing more. The reason Fido shot J. T. is because he was about to kill Jim Bruno in a land-grabbing scheme. They tentatively were buying that part of the story until further checking could be done. Fido let the fallen trees go unexplained as some kind of williwaw wind that had kicked up during the storm. Trees fell on power lines around Anchor Point all the time, but never in one place. Strangely, the weather cleared up once the troopers arrived. Understandably, they were skeptical, shaking their heads. Fido would not budge, and at last they relented. Jim and Fido were cleared.

"That's good to hear, Fido. Thanks."

"Jimmy, my boy, for you anytime."

The door opened again and there stood Dr. Dan greeting them all. He moved to Ed's bedside in doctor fashion, shone a light into Ed's eyes and took his pulse. Satisfied, he came around and put a hand out to Fido.

"Well, hello, Fido. How have you been?"

Jesus! Jim thought, is there anybody Fido doesn't already know?

"Just fine, Doc. Things been a little hectic lately though." Fido winked at Jim. "You taking good care of these boys for me?"

"Yes." The doctor lifted Bruno's chart from the end of the bed. Being overly formal to his disabled friend, Dr. Dan remarked, "Mr. Bruno, your femur is broken. How did you manage that?"

"Drill stem fell on me, Doc," Jim said lamely.

"Hmmmm...I guess I'll have to get Mr. Tasker to tell me all about it on his way out." And with that Fido found himself being willingly escorted from the premises.

"Oh, yeah!" Fido stopped with one hand on the doorknob. "Some little squatty-body bald-headed guy named. ..Aston?. ..Alton?... Yeah! Alton! Came by with some buddies of his. A couple of Natives and I think a guy from Fairbanks. They wanted to get into your customers' place. Troopers wouldn't let 'um in. Said they'd be back in the morning and, I dunno.. .do something. They weren't real talkative."

Lucky for us, Jim thought. "Was the customer out there, Fido?"

"Uh-huh. The cops went out and found them down at the boat harbor. I guess his fishing boat damn near sank. Right in its slip! Appears somebody pulled the dry-dock plug!"

Dr. Dan was pulling on Fido's arm now, with little effect.

"Okay, Doc, okay. Jimmy, I'll send one of the kids down to drill that cement outta there for ya, all right?"

"Thanks a million, Fido!" How could he ever repay his old friend for all this?

"Sokay, see ya later!"

After the excitement of Jim explaining to Ed what went on out at the job and Fido's visit, uncomfortable silences intruded between Jim and Ed. The two stared vacantly out the hospital window at the twinkling lights on the Homer Spit.

Ed seemed to be suppressing his emotions. Jim knew Ed didn't blame him or harbor any ill will. Probably nervous about his future, going through the rest of his life minus a foot. Ed had to be wondering: Will I be able to walk? Will I look funny trying? How will I drive a car? What about swimming? Will I ever get laid again?

Jim hoped Ed still wanted to drill when he got out of the hospital. Before this happened Jim had been thinking of making Ed a limited partner. When Ed jumped in to fight the rig fire that day out on the highway without any regard for his personal safety, it was clinched.

Soft snoring told him Ed's painkillers had taken effect.

Jim, on the other hand, had a tough time falling asleep. He supposed he should be celebrating the culmination of this "well from hell." The thin hospital blanket wasn't enough cover to shield him from the self-doubt and confusion coming in on him now.

Mistaken. Fooled. Bushwhacked.

He failed to see J. T. coming. He should have never let himself get blind-sided like that.

And what did Alton want to do tomorrow?

Jim had witnessed many lines being crossed today. Even the line separating life from death. Just thinking, doubting, questioning his accountability in today's events was pushing Jim perilously close to a line he didn't want to be near.

Whooommp!

That noise. The first couple of times his eyelids got heavy, the sound of the fuel tanker exploding or the screech of the Yaku-beast would jerk him awake. Jim was beginning to understand, this might take some time to get over.

Jim slept fitfully, dividing the night between dreaming and a semiconscious state. He was somewhat aware of a nurse opening the door two or three times allowing an immersion of hallway lighting to flood the room before exiting softly. When dreaming, he heard and saw his late father scolding him fervently about being responsible.

Bruno was the first of the two men to wake. He lay quietly looking out the window, his skin under the cast itching like mad. He was thinking about trying to get up and find a coat hanger to straighten out when the door opened tentatively. A nurse's fortyish eyes sparkled at him, her body yet to be seen.

She quietly said, "Jim, you have a phone call. Shall I put it through?" Did he know her? He couldn't recall. With a nod from Jim, she left. Less than a minute passed before the telephone light started blinking. "Hello?"

"Jim Bruno?"

Instantly recognizable, the deep voice of Professor Dan Alton made itself at home in Jim's imagination.

"Professor. How are you?"

"I am fine. I fear it is I who should be asking the question. Are you all right? I gather you experienced some astonishing events yesterday."

"I saw it professor. I saw it kill someone."

"You saw...Yaku?" The professor's voice exhaled.

"No.. Yes... I mean, I don't know. This thing that killed Darrell then came after us looked like the kiki..."

"Kikituk?"

"Yeah, like the kikituk you showed me a picture of in your classroom. Only this thing was way bigger."

"Bigger?"

"Oh, man, was it ever. Professor, this thing had eyes identical to the one in the picture, but it stood four or five feet tall. It was very strong. It chased us out to the road after we shot it, and it was still alive after a tractor-trailer ran it over. It didn't die until the whole ball of wax was engulfed in a huge fireball."

Silence.

"Professor Alton? Are you still there?"

"Yes, Jim. Could you hold a moment?"

Jim could hear past the muffled mouthpiece of Alton's phone, but only enough to tell he was talking to someone, nothing more. Jim's ear was becoming weary of having the phone pressed to it when the professor spoke up again.

"Jim, Ben Jamison and the two practicing shamans from the north slope villages arrived late yesterday. Unfortunately, too late to be permitted into the site. Jim, it is imperative that these men be allowed on the property today to ensure Yaku's power has been completely eviscerated! Can you arrange it?"

"I...I think so. Yes. Professor, call me back in half an hour." Jim still couldn't call the man by his first name. "I'll get ahold of the customer and see if it's okay for us to meet out there."

"Very well then. Good-bye."

Am I crazy? Why did I say I'd go back out there? Jim shook his head at himself. Guess it's like getting back up on the horse that threw you, and after all, we do still have a drill rig out there and we still need to set a pump, don't we? Jim chided himself for being a chicken. What the hell did eviscerated mean anyway? He wasn't certain he wanted to find out.

Jim called the nurses' station next. "Yes" he was told, "You will be released this morning but Dr. White wants to see you before signing you out."

Jim hung up with a finger, head tilted, receiver between chin and shoulder. After dialing Moss's, Jim listened to the unanswered rings, biting his bottom lip, trying to foresee the conversation.

"Hello?" It was Sam.

"Sam, it's Jim. How you folks holding up out there?"

"Jim!" He sounded excited to be hearing from Jim. "We're okay. The place is kind of a mess though. But hey! How are you? From what the troopers told us, J. T. tried to kill you so he could get our land! Is that true? They said a brown bear mauled Darrell Klepesen! Man, oh man! We haven't had anything but black bears around here for a long time!"

Waiting to get a word in, Jim looked in Ed's direction and found him to be bleary-eyed, but awake, listening. Jim leaned his head back in greeting. Ed managed a smile in return.

"I'm fine, Sam. Yes, that's pretty much what happened. Say, did anyone tell you I hit water, lots of it, right before all hell broke loose?"

"What?"

They didn't know. Fido had not told them so Jim could have the pleasure.

"Yep. Like at least twenty-five gallons a minute. I couldn't bail it down! Hit it at 250 feet."

"ALLLLLRIGHT!" Relief gushed into Jim's ear via the receiver. Ed had a big sappy grin on his face.

Jim could overhear Sam call "Annie. We got water!" followed by an excited shriek in the background.

"That's great news, Jim! Fantastic! We were told J. T. wanted our land for the oil under it. Without water we were just discussing having to sell. Don't believe we will now. Your big burly friend was here to ask us if he could park his pickup. He said you had something to tell us, we were hoping but..."

"Sam, did anything strange happen last night? I mean, after they took J. T. and Darrell away and everyone left?"

"No, why?"

"Professor Alton from the community college called me this morning. Some experts from Fairbanks are in town. They would like to come out to your place. Make sure it's safe."

"Does this have something to do with all the trees being knocked down?"

"Yes."

"That wasn't no brown bear that killed Darrell, was it?"

"No."

"The troopers found Annies' cat out by where Darrell got attacked, something killed it, didn't look like no bear ate it though." Sam paused "What time will you be out, Jim?"

Now Jim was guessing. "Sometime around noon. Also, there may a kid from Soldotna showing up to do a little clean-out drilling. Can you keep an eye on him for me 'til we get there? I don't want anything to happen to him."

"Sure, Jim. I'll cut that tree off your rig for him."

Jim cringed. "Okay, but please be careful. The professor sounded concerned."

On the other end of the phone line, Sam hung up in slow motion, considering everything Jim had said. Then the five-gallon buckets caught his eye, and he just smiled at them.

Again Jim hung up with his finger and redialed. He heard an enthusiastic "hello!" right after the first ring.

"Jester! Are ya up?"

"Roger that, Jimbo! Reveille for me is at oh-dark-thirty! What's your status? Sounds like you'll be getting a purple heart!"

Good old Jess. "I'm fine, Jess, But I don't think I can drive. I need a lift out to Moss's today. Are you hooked up?"

"That's affirmative. But I'll go AWOL!" Jess cackled gleefully. A rule-breaking buck private again.

"Can you be here at eleven?"

"Ten-four."

"See you then, Jess, thanks."

The professor called and it was set. They would all meet at Moss's at noon.

God. Would anything happen out there today? Ed looked at his boss. They were both wondering the same thing.

"Jim?"

"Yeah?"

"Could you thank Annie for me?"

Jim smiled, "Be glad to."

The weather improved remarkably for the drive out to Moss's. The town of Anchor Point seemed alive again. Normal hustling and bustling resumed. People seemed to be happy.

"What's everybody saying, Jess?" Until now they rode in silence, Jess leaving Jim to his thoughts.

"Well, mostly they are surprised about J. T. being a section eight over money. Everyone knew he was greedy, but this... this caught all personnel with their flanks open. The hotel and bar closed yesterday, supposed to be open again today." That emblazoned the seriousness of the situation. The Silver-King lodge never closed. It was even open on Christmas. Only on election days, by law, during chamber of commerce meetings, and once a year for the employees' Christmas party did the bar ever shut down.

"Nobody's saying anything bad about you, Jimmy. If they did I'd give 'em a knuckle sandwich." Jess made a fist with his left hand. "Fact is, you're a half-assed hero. Rumor has it you might have got some water out there."

"Yeah, I did. lots of it."

"Outstanding. Sam and Annie must be tickled."

Jim returned to his introspection. What does it take to cause a person to cross the line and go so evil that he harms his fellow man without conscience? Jake Bantam did it, presumably Yaku had done it too, years ago. Jim thought crossing this line much different from crossing others. Maybe it's the premeditation that made it so... blatant, so hard to swallow. Was simple greed enough to do it? Fate? What?

Jim Bruno, his leg sticking uncomfortably straight out in the cab of Jester's truck, wondered what, if anything, would cause him to become really violent. What if someone burned down the house he'd built with his own two hands on the beach? What if someone raped a loved one? Murdered his mom? What would it take?

Bruno snapped back to reality. He and Jess passed the charred area along the highway, testimony to what happened yesterday.

Jess whistled. "Looks like artillery hit this place."

Jester wheeled the work truck off the highway onto Moss's road without using the turn signal. Part way down the gravel road, they came upon the full-grown birch that fell across the road. It was now in three pieces to allow traffic to pass. The closer Big Jim got to yesterday's incidents, the more explicit the memory became. He felt his resolve to be part of this diminishing. Tugging to get away like a skiff pulling against loose moorings.

Driving into Moss's to park, it seemed they were the last to arrive. A small crowd was grouped in front of the log house. Fido's pickup caught Jim's eye. His heart lifted. Then he remembered the condition Fido's truck was in after they went ditch diving. It was parked on a type of dead rail next to Roy-Boy's bashed-in M. V. Obviously Fido had left it there until it could be repaired or towed. Jim made a mental note to take care of it.

"Can you operate them implements?" Jess asked jokingly, nodding to the crutches between them.

"Never have tried to find out." The nurses had pushed Jim out to the hospital parking lot in a wheelchair.

Jim leaned way to the left before he had the necessary room needed to manipulate his straight leg out the truck's door. He propped himself up with his good leg and shortly after, he was standing, though painfully.

Jess handed Big Jim the crutches out of the truck door. Jim hoped he wouldn't wipe out in front of all these people.

The crutches took a step, then Jim swung through, landing on his good foot. Okay!

Professor Alton was the first to step forward and shake Jim's hand. The professor seemed excited. To Alton's right were the men from out of town.

One was a distinguished-looking man, tall, thin, with straight black hair and glasses that looked the same as Alton's. He was the type that always seemed to be taking mental notes. He reached over to shake Jim's hand while Alton introduced him as Ben Jamison. He had a very weak handshake, which always made Jim a little queasy. Maybe Mr. Jamison was just being careful not to injure Jim further.

Next, Dan Alton introduced the two elderly Natives. Small in stature, they seemed perfectly content to be standing there, waiting. They didn't offer hands as Alton introduced them. Rather than shake, they simply leaned their chests forward, nodded their heads, and smiled politely. Bruno forgot their names almost immediately, partly because he was so surprised by their appearance.

They both had mukluks on their feet, but other than that they wore no traditional Eskimo clothing. No headdresses, no painted faces. Jim laughed at himself for expecting voodoo priests.

The elder of the two shamans wore an Oakland Raiders' jacket one size too big for him. He was very thin, to the point of seeming frail. The deeply wrinkled flesh on his face hung loose, past his jaw line. He was toothless. His lips were large and soft-looking. His eyes bugged out slightly and appeared watery.

The younger of the pair wore thick gray pants and a parka with Russian Orthodox embroidery around the borders and fur all the way around every edge, from hood to bottom, even the cuffs. His face was rounded. He looked like he'd led a good life up to now.

To save going through more introductions, Jess just sort of hung back and tried to act like he knew everyone.

The younger shaman lifted the doctor's bag that was on the ground by his side. Everyone followed them as they headed down in the direction of the well.

Sam and Annie came around behind the group where Jim was. Big Bruno rubbed his chin. He needed a shave. He must look pretty rough.

Sam shook his hand firmly. Annie gave him a one-arm hug. They started down, bringing up the rear again.

"Are you getting hit with the same deja vu as I am?" Annie asked Jim. Jim smiled yes.

Halfway to the rig, the front group stopped. The younger shaman leaned over to Jamison, said something and set the bag down. He leaned over it and began working his hands inside.

Ben Jamison turned to the rest of the group and said, "If the power of Yaku is still here, it is too faint or dormant for them to detect. Yaku could be lingering, however. They will try to force him out. They will perform a ceremony, much like an exorcism."

"Is that a good idea?" Jim almost said out loud.

The round-faced shaman removed a long cloth from the doctor's bag. He whipped his hands back one at a time as each protective layer unfolded. Revealed was a short staff, intricately adorned with fish bone, beads, and seal fur.

The elder shaman also took a turn reaching into the bag. He removed a small hand drum with the face of a bird carved on its top.

The two old men started walking again, this time much slower, the elder of the two banging on the drum in no particular rhythm, both men making low guttural sounds. Jim couldn't tell if they were words or chants. There were a lot of rolling k's, uk's, and t's. It sounded somewhat like someone preparing to spit, hawking up phlegm.

The younger shaman was holding the staff out in front of him like a.. like *a witching rod.*

Jim opened his mouth to comment but thought better of it. This job had come full circle, with these Eskimo witchers out here now. Only they were witching in reverse, withching to get rid of somethjing, not discover something.

"Yaku could be lingering" was what the man said. Damn, let's hope not, thought Jim. The two men were almost to the rig now, their entourage just behind.

A low rumble started. It became louder very fast. The ground shook. Worried looks were traded all around. It seemed a full-scale earthquake was about to begin.

"Most amazing," Alton exclaimed.

"Quite," his associate Jamison agreed.

Jim's first instinct was to look up at the derrick. It didn't seem to be moving. Man, if it came down....

As soon as all the others had their hands outstretched from their sides for balance, the shaking stopped.

In that immediate moment, Jim fleetingly thought he had the meaning of life within his grasp, on the tip of his brain. It wasn't anything he could put into words, just a feeling. Like when you have a barely discernible thought pass through your mind. As though when a person passes you on a crowded street, you think you may know them. Upon realizing you don't, you forget they even passed by at all.

Yes. It came back to him. The source of all life forces comes from nature, which nurtures us all. When Mother Nature becomes hostile to us, we perish. When she is kind, we thrive and prosper. The only people in tune with this are not the popes or the presidents or the kings, but people who are in tune with the Earth. Like shamans, dowsers, rainmakers and anyone that understands good and evil both come from one place, Mother Earth.

"Jim? Are you all right?" Annie had a concerned look on her face.

"Oh, yeah, I'm fine." Thanks for snapping me out of it, Jim thought.

The two old Natives and the two professors were engaged in a hushed conference.

"Annie, Ed asked me to thank you."

"You spoke with him? How is he?" she asked.

"We were in the same room at the hospital. He's grateful to you."

"You tell him I'll be bringing a big batch of muffins tomorrow."

"You got it."

The four men were now walking toward them with Alton leading the way.

The professor said to them, "It seems we're concluded."

"That's it? All the way from the slope for that, huh?" Sam asked him.

"Yes. They will stop at the site of Yaku's incineration, mostly a formality, I believe. There was little left of Yaku and now he has been completely vanquished.

"Reverse witching," Jim thought.

"Professor, will yo be asking to resume the dig, now that this has been found out?" Sam asked.

"No." Alton answered without hesitation.

Sam and Annie invited everyone in for a crab quiche lunch and to thank them all for coming. While they were inside, one of Tasker's sons arrived, cranked up Jim's rig and started drilling out the cement.

Pound-growl. ..Pound-growl...Pound-growl. Soon Jim was on his way home with Jester.

"Jess, you think this cast will get me any sympathy drinks at the lodge?"

"Roger that!"

"You mind stopping?"

"Hell no!"

Jim didn't really want to drink. There was another reason he wanted to go to the bar.

The mood inside the bar was strange. A mixture of relief and mourning prevailed. Jim accepted kudos and pats on the back.

She was there, bouncing and bopping as always. She smiled at him with those big beautiful round eyes. Jim planned what he was going to say, but he was losing it. His heart was beating faster and he was having a hard time breathing normally.

When Tripoli headed over to feed the jukebox, he saw his chance. By the time he had crutched his way over to her, she had picked out all the songs the bartender asked for.

"Hi, Jim! Want to pick a couple? There's still two left."

"No. You go ahead. Trip, I..."

She looked at him, waiting. At that point Jim almost bailed out. He was flirting with crossing the line that separates loneliness from companionship. With his heart up around the base of his throat, he finally asked her.

"Trip, what do you think of me?"

Trippi answered without hesitation. "I like you, Jim." she said, blinking one beautiful eye closed, with the other looking up to her forehead as if reading what was on her mind. She continued, "I think you're like a big ol' goose egg. Someone needs to sit on you and warm you up a bit so we can hatch you and see what's inside."

Sounds like a plan. "When I get off these crutches, I'll come visit you, 'kay?"

"Why wait?"

Why indeed.

GLOSSARY OF TERMS

Bump Uglies—Have sexual intercourse.

Cache—A place (usually a cabin on stilts) where stores of food, supplies, etc., are hidden and kept safe from animals.

Faller—The lumberjack who actually cuts down the trees with a chain saw.

Gangions (pronounced gan-yens)—Quick connecting clasps that have a short piece of line attached to them with a hook on the end. The hook is then baited, and the gangions are slapped onto a long line as it is spooled off of a boat's reel into the water. The long line is kept on the bottom for several hours by anchors at each end, then pulled out, back onto the reel, and any hooked fish harvested.

Gill-netters—Commercial fishermen who fish salmon by stretching a 900-foot net out behind their boat. The net is kept afloat by buoys, and is weighted at its bottom by a lead line. The salmon swimming into the net are trapped by the gills, the holes in the net that are just large enough for their heads.

Muskeg—Wet openings found between forest stands of bog plant communities growing on deep peat, dominated by sphagnum moss, sedges, rushes, and shrubs. Sparse tree growth consists of hemlock and lodgepole pine in scrub form. Habitat for many plants. Provides stream flow and home for wildlife. Found over much of the Alaska.

North Slope—The Brooks Range stretches across northern Alaska above the Arctic circle, gradually sloping northward to the Arctic ocean and the Beaufort Sea. Hence the nickname " the slope."

Oh-dark thirty—Army slang for *very* early, as in oh-five hundred (five A.M.) but before sunrise.

Slack (or ebb) tide—The point at which high tide stops coming up but has not yet begun to recede, or, the point where mean low tide is all the way out and has yet to begin to rise.

Slope widows—Women whose husbands are away for weeks at a time working in the oil fields north of the Brooks Range at Prudhoe Bay, Endicott, or Kuparuk.

Williwaw—A violent, cold wind blowing in far northern latitudes.

Bill Fry is a 20-year Alaskan. In his life he has worked as a cook, a bartender, and has stomped jugs on a seismic crew. He has done marine salvage work and spent the last nine years working in the oil fields of Prudhoe Bay and Kuparuk. For seventeen years, he owned and operated a water-well drilling business in Anchor Point and Homer, Alaska. This book is based, in part, on his experiences. He curently lives in Homer with his wife, Dorothy, and their two daughters.

I apologize to Native Alaskan Eskimos and Indians for taking liberties with their heritage and geography. Please remember this is a work of fiction, meant only to entertain.

Thank you, Susie Wohlgemuth, for being such an awesome editor. You took something raw and made it so much better than it was. Thanks also to the boys in Prudhoe: Rex Spore, Takbuk, Big Dick Beck, Dan Lewis, Don Chenault, Moss and Wrongway. Good friends all. You helped more than you know. Thanks to J.R. Baldwin for convincing me I had enough material. Thanks to everyone that had a good enough sense of humor to let me use their name in the story. And deep appreciation to Jan O'Meara for making a real book out of this.

And, of course, thank you, Dorothy, for your support and encouragement. I love you.

For other books about Alaska contact

Wizard Works
Publisher of Books about Alaska and
The Alaska Small Press Catalog
P.O. Box 1125
Homer, AK 99603
ph/fax (907) 235-5305

Paws IV Publishing
P.O. Box 2364
Homer, AK 99603
ph. 1-800-807-PAWS
fax (907) 235-7698